Cameron Redfern is the pseudonym of a writer who lives in Melbourne.

'Forensic in its dissection of sexual obsession and, towards the end, the blistering consequences of getting involved with a married man' *Sydney Morning Herald*

'This is such good writing. It is the work of someone who loves words, who loves writing and reading, who understands how language works and how words can be put together to touch the heart and the mind and make the reader glad that there are still people in the world who can do this' *Australian*

LANDSCAPE WITH ANIMALS

Cameron Redfern

virago

VIRAGO

First published in Great Britain in 2007 by Virago Press
Reprinted 2012

First published in Australia in 2006 by the Penguin Group (Australia),
a division of Pearson Australia Group Pty Ltd.

A CIP catalogue record for this book
is available from the British Library.

ISBN 978-1-84408-445-6

Typeset in Sabon by M Rules
Printed and bound in Great Britain by Clays Ltd, St Ives plc

Papers used by Virago are from well-managed forests
and other responsible sources.

MIX
Paper from
responsible sources
FSC® C104740

Virago Press
An imprint of
Little, Brown Book Group
100 Victoria Embankment
London EC4Y 0DY

An Hachette UK Company
www.hachette.co.uk

www.virago.co.uk

*Love that moves the
sun and the other stars.*

DANTE

She knows his name before she knows him, a name like an intricate puzzle made from stainless steel; it's a name she's heard often, and written down sometimes, but their paths have never intersected, and she has never hoped they would. She's prone to invention from thin air, and when she gives him any thought it is coloured by the cool untouchable silveriness of his name. She does not picture him as a man who laughs, who can take and make a joke: from the innocuous letters of his name alone she cobbles a personality that is austere, mannerly, antisocial. She's antisocial herself, sees nothing wrong with the trait, admires it even; but she has no desire to meet him. When he crosses her mind it is on a ribbon of resentment, that in

———

all the years she's traipsed their common circles he has never sought her out, never given her his time, never paid her the attention she's been led to believe she's due. There is nothing she can do about it except to give him little thought in return.

So when they do meet, in a crowded room, she is amazed.

He's not so tall as she had devised; much more finely-boned. She's brought to face him grudgingly and in exchange he gives her only a polished glimpse of his regard: he leans down to her in the way she detests, she speaks in a tone of ingratiating sunniness that he doubtlessly loathes, both of them radiate the barest grip on civility – but standing in his shadow she feels some-thing like a tidal wave haul through her, something like a flock of birds erupting into the air. *You're beautiful*, she thinks: he's the most strangely beautiful man she has ever seen. He has a jackal's lankiness, a poetry to his face. He doesn't say he is pleased to meet her; his voice is clipped, he hardly smiles. He gives the impression of impatience habitually and barely contained. Yet she knows, just standing there, the birds calling inside her, that he will be one of the great loves of her life. She sees it as if it's carved in timeless mountains, as if she's been born with her destiny tattooed on her skin: he will be, maybe, the very greatest. And when, as convention insists, she must step away, seep into the crowd, return him to the conversation he'd had to interrupt, she doesn't bother glancing back. His image is cut in her.

That night she lies in her dusty bed alone, her knees splayed and her palm pressed hard against her pubic bone. She is a girl who loves to fuck – a dirty girl, she sometimes thinks, because the description amuses her. She has a vein of gushing, uncultured, sensually bad blood. But there has been no one for months – no one, ever, in this house. She's lived a penitent's life since she came here, to this silent suburb where widows live out the scrap-ends of their lives and trees grow to majestic heights. But at night she's sometimes visited by a secretive stealthy heat that drives up into her, an arrogant force that fucks her from the inside out and vanishes with a dismissiveness when it's done with her, leaving her boneless on the bed, her cunt throbbing, her breathing shallow. She's never been ashamed of this creature that comes – she adores it, she's grateful. Its visits

———

remind her that she is, not very far underneath the surface, a creature herself. When she was young she had watched the brutal and enthusiastic matings of the animals she kept – mice and cats, vicious rapists who tore at one another screechingly, sinking their fangs into scruffs. Dogs, with their sweet courtship, their fearsome grip on each other; afterwards they did not want to part, they could not, their fucking became bondage. She had watched her pets furtively, her cunt wetting even as a little girl: she longed to have her legs parted, to have something warm living rigid driven into her. It was then, as a child, that she'd understood she was animal. Her pets knew how to fuck, were born wanting to: she was the same. And she liked this bestial core of herself, this raw and avaricious thing; liked, even, its scorn of her attempts to please herself. When she pushed her fingers inside, she shared its contempt. An animal, she craved the base – she needed the fervency of another, to be weighed down sweatily, passionately handled, bitten and injured. She needed to feel, the following day, the gouges left by a cock run assertively into her. Lying on her bed, her thoughts unpicking the details of him, her fingers dither over the tacky flesh of her

4

cunt, but she doesn't enter herself in his name. He will fuck her himself. She doesn't think of his cock, or the sight of his naked body: she imagines the pressure of his chest, his gasping in her ear, his racing heart, his uncontrolled cursing, the minutes when he will be hers. The catch, the kill. She is not just an animal: she is a predator, and she will run him down. Her affection is a boundlessly tender but inexorably determined thing. She will snare him in claws like seductive sunlight; numbed by shock, he won't feel anything but the desire to offer his throat.

Her need for him is urgent, but she steps painstakingly. She casts out his name and listens to what people say, probing what she hears for weaknesses and joys. No one, she finds, knows much about him – she feels from a distance his reserve, how rarely his subject is himself. Nobody's world is an ordinary place, she knows – yet she's told only mundane things about him, facts she could have guessed, information on the mainstays of his existence, which is useless to her. What she's hunting are the small things – the kindnesses he might appreciate, the opinions that go unheard, the pleasures he's forgotten or relinquished. He must have a soft underbelly beneath his

————

steely shell: he's bound to have sorrows, wants, regrets. He must be taken for granted; he must feel rusted into place. In her eyes, though, he will shine: he'll emanate a gorgeous glow. He will find, in her, everything he thought was irretrievably gone. She will rise in his world like a star.

Through summer and autumn she works on her house, lacquering the floorboards, pulling up carpets, skimming across the roof. She digs the soil, heaps gardenbeds, plants saplings, envisages them grown. There is much to be done, painting, building, tearing down. At all times he is with her, in a corner of her mind. He knows her name now, the places she can be found. They talk on the telephone. At first he rang just occasionally, as a grounded guardian angel would, when things were going wrong for her, when she felt alone; soon he phones almost every day, and his reasons for doing so become flimsy. They talk of their work, their travels, what they have in common. The elements that make their lives so different are the subjects they hedge around. Sometimes she thinks she's bored him, or sallied unwisely far; but he soon returns, resilient, laughing off her apologies. They laugh together more and more. He sends her trinkets he thinks she'll like, a chocolate, a toy, a book – she studies his scraggly writing, plumbing the depths of a casually crossed kiss. They compare invitations, enquiring if the other means to go; she buys new clothes if she thinks they'll be sharing the same space. He orchestrates occasions for lunch; she insists on splitting the bill. She's playful in his shade, trotting along puppishly, showing off the things she can do. She touches his arm, the small of his back, so he hardly knows it's done. She's learning the smell of him, the precise colour of his eyes. Every time she sees him, she's thrown by how striking he is; she envies the very air he breathes. She talks about him to everyone and they hear the rising of her voice, the increasing momentousness of the thing, and she is warned off by them all. *It is you who'll have your heart destroyed.* She shrugs it aside – she knows she mustn't get too fond, she's willing to free him when she should. He might be her greatest love, but that doesn't mean he feels the same. But she won't think about the end, when everything has scarcely begun. For now, she is racing full speed to the brink of a precipice, unstoppable.

At the beginning of spring they go to a party, not together, but because they know the other will be there.

———

She leans in a doorway, a shoulder against the frame, her eyes on her glass because he stands before her saying nothing, shy as a calf. She knows that tonight will change things, and maybe he knows it too. She has reached the edge, and tonight she will fly or fall. She's bought a shirt that dips between her breasts – he gives no sign of noticing. Sometimes she thinks she has failed spectacularly, that he is blind to the glimmerance in her eyes – that she was, perhaps, always bound to fail, because he has no daring, because he is, unconquerably, an honourable man. She will want to hit him; she'll want to storm off sobbing. It will make her furious, saying goodbye.

They aren't alone. The party is loud and crowded, and people want to speak with him, so he must continuously look away; but he stays near her, his gaze returns to her. They exchange frivolities in those moments when it's just he and she. She's drunk enough to tip on her toes, but her thoughts are crisp as birdsong. She glances at him, and his eyes are on her. She can scarcely look at him. She wants to fuck this quiet man until he cries: fuck him in cars, in laneways, in playgrounds at midnight as if they're seventeen. She'd take his cock and suck until he roared; she'd

---

take his hand and press it to her stomach so he could feel himself moving in her. She'd fuck him on beaches, park benches, in bed, in the rain; fuck him without boundaries, upside-down, back-to-front, up her arse, up his own. She would smooth his brow, trace his lips, brush his cheek, whisper to him, she'd close his pretty eyes beneath her palms. She would make him swear to die for her, if only she knew how. Instead she hears herself saying, in her charmless, cheapest voice: 'You know, don't you, that I want to screw you until you scream?'

It is uncouth and blundering, repulsively juvenile, almost knocks her to her knees: but he doesn't recoil, he doesn't even blink. And she has a thought that nearly smites her: *he has heard such things before.* He's not startled, because he is one of those irritating men over whom women war like crows. And she feels brokenly stupid, to have fallen for such a man: she'd prefer never to desire, than to desire unoriginally. Disgraced, she plunges inward, meaning to rifle through what little she knows about stylish retreats: and finds, to her surprise, a lioness crouched within her, her coat battle-scarred but golden, her tail heavily swatting the air. A lion to stand beside her.

———

She smiles off-handedly, says, 'I bet you hear that line every day.'

'Hardly,' he says.

She looks up, searching his face for honesty – he isn't smiling, she'll remember that. 'Really?' She speaks with care. 'You should. We should.'

'I would if I could,' he says, 'but I can't.'

Her gaze skids, her heart springs at the words, yet she's wary of making herself a greater fool – she won't swallow rebuffing lies. But he's standing still, frowning, he doesn't seem to breathe. Her eyes coast the jostling court-yard and return to him. 'Why can't?' she asks.

He holds up a hand, shows her his fingers. She would like to touch them, bend them inside hers, taste them at her lips. Instead she shrugs disdainfully: 'So? You didn't ask my opinion before you did that. Why punish me for something I had no say in?'

He laughs at this, smothers it. He's bumped from behind, shifts his footing, nods curtly to someone who greets him. When he looks again at her, she says, 'I don't want to keep you. I only want to borrow you. I'll send you home in one piece. No strings.'

———

'I'd like it,' he says hushly, and it's a knife to the chest, because she believes him. 'I've thought about it. I can't, though. I couldn't. You should forget me, concentrate on your work. I would only disappoint you. You can find somebody better.'

The music is loud, welling up behind her, but she doesn't raise her voice. 'I don't want somebody better. I want you. From the moment I saw you, I only wanted you.'

He stares at the courtyard cobbles, hands tight around his glass. 'I'm flattered,' he says. 'I'm sorry. I would if I could. I'm sorry I can't.'

She nods, smiles evenly, as a good loser might: when she pulls her hooks out of him she hopes she leaves weeping wounds. The party continues, but she doesn't stay long. They drift apart, away from the doorway, both of them find others to talk to. She isn't angry, but she's hollow: there's nothing to be done. She doesn't remember giving him another glance.

Only later, alone, undressed in her bed, she muses on what he'd said. *I've thought about it.* The words smell like timber or vanilla. *I would if I could but I can't.* It makes almost no sense to her – she rarely disallows herself any thing that she wants. She's keenly aware of living just once. She's aware of answering to no one, that there is only she. No one waiting, wondering about her, no one claiming her.

She ponders the ceiling, arms folded under her head, her pillows tipped to the floor. She remembers the flick of the lioness's tail, the rasp of her tongue over teeth. She should be gracious, she should feel humiliated, at the very least be defeated: but she is none of these. He had said something else to her: *concentrate on your work*. Her work is to manipulate, invent, instil. Her job is to conjure something out of nothing. To force belief; to create what could be.

At four in the morning she gets out of bed and writes to him, linking word after word.

———

They will always be a story, she writes, *and the story will always be about him.* All, everything, him—

She'd told him no strings, *as if she doesn't know that the world is tied together with string, that everything hangs poised from thread; that string, tied tight enough, slices to bone. Of course she knows it – how impossible it is, to avoid the hideous knots – but she is resolved. When he wants it to end, she will go. She can't begrudge him his need to keep his world intact. It's wrong to ask him to risk the things that make his life fulfilling. And she's vowed never to speak, afterward, of the terrible ruinous death-plunge that comes with the cutting of strings.*

That day – the last day – is always there, swirling beneath them like ash. Every day demands they step with agility. They are like diamond-cutters – cautious, examining detail, feeling in their minds the shape of what lies beneath. Yet there are also times of ridiculous excitement, when he turns handstands, when she runs as fast as she can, when they feel six years old on Christmas morning, when they know how it is to have wings. He wonders if he isn't becoming addicted to this feeling. He doesn't love her – he scorns the notion of love at first sight, of loving one hardly known, for life must have scale, some things must be earned – but he loves the divine taste of this fresh-minted euphoria. It's what he will miss most when the last day comes and nothing returns to normal.

She won't take him to her house. At the end, there should be a place in her life where he hasn't been. So she fucks him on the spongy seats of her car, in public parkland close to busy roads, in rubbish-blown lanes and carparks, in sidestreets near his home. A man accustomed to gentleness, at first these stark places alarmed him; but his aversion to dingy haunts disappeared one night when the sky was slate with city lights and she led him down a bluestone alley and turned her face to the wall. He'd fucked her with his arms crossed between her breasts and his belt buckle clinking, the noise of horns and arguments rising from nearby. His hands had parted the groove of her arse, his fingers had combed through damp hair: he'd pulled her close and thrust into her hard, wincing at her narrow depths. His heart, as always, had been crashing in his chest, frightened, appalled, quickened by need. Moments from coming, his breathing loud to his ears, he had glanced up to see a cat standing on a fence-top, motionless as only a stray can be, its colourless eyes considering him. He'd been jolted by surprise – he had never been watched by a wild animal before – and suddenly he understood about these furtive places she seemed to prefer. There was nothing about this – about the two of them, what they were doing – that was dignified: but every black corner was theirs. And he, whose life has been lived in the light, has begun to see such places everywhere. At his desk, in whitest sunshine, he daydreams about darkness.

One evening they both attend a cocktail party in the grounds of a fabulous house. The night is fragrant, the moon is low. The air is dense with chatter, laughter, glass on glass, mosquitoes delicate as calligraphy. The food is tastefully Japanese. The exhibiting artists are cooed over, then genteelly stabbed in the back. He is aware of her presence at the edge of the crowd, perched cross-legged on a stone wall. She is talking to a handsome man whose name he can't recall. He sees her touch this man with a finger – she is a ceaseless flirt. He used to like it, her being so – he liked thinking of her as a sharp-toothed, mean little beast over whose behaviour he had no control. Now, though, he is changing. He doesn't love her, but he doesn't want her loving anyone else. And he feels the pull of a string strong enough to easily hang a man.

The speeches are given, the exhibition is launched, the gathering shifts gear. The handsome man continues to sit with her, near enough for their elbows to touch. It's a relief when somebody else joins them; somebody else, as well. He crosses the lawn and smiles down at her. 'Hello.'

'There are never any cocktails at cocktail parties,' she announces, mostly drunk.

He introduces himself to the handsome man. He won't forget the name again. He sips wine and talks to the people around her, a master at being interested in everyone: her, *he ignores. It's only as he's moving away that he bends to say something close to her ear.*

The house has acres of garden, most of it tidy and formal – but there is a forest planted by a long-gone owner who loved the land and earthly things, a place for webs and owls, a wild lightless corner far removed from the rooftops and pebble paths that surround it. The trees rise up in shambling blackness and seem unfriendly, there's a faint suggestion of peril. It is, impeccably, one of their places; and it's easy for them to drift into it, to take a step beyond the party lamps and be in darkness, to take another and be gone.

She slips her fingers between his, which is rare. Rare too is the fact that she wears a dress – he knows she is doing it for him. It's the only concession she's made, how-ever – she is not by nature girly. She wears underwear like a schoolboy's, lolly-coloured bras without frill. She stops with her back against a treetrunk, moonshine streaking her face. They can still hear the party, but it's inconse-quential to them. He bends to kiss her, her forehead and mouth. They have learned not to talk. The material of her dress is flimsy, ethereal in his hands. He hooks his fingers

————

in her underwear, rolls them down her thighs. Her legs are all muscle, she has a kick like a mule, yet she stands demurely on her very tiptoes. He presses close, exploring the scratchy edges of her cunt, the folds and coy places there. She sighs, closing her eyes. When he slots two fingers into her she stiffens, her wrists knock the tree. She feels more than warm inside. He's fallen in adolescent love with this snug space that holds him, its slick invitation, its obliging ways. He dips his fingers in and out, coating them in her balm. His fingers reach up into her, two, three, as far as he is allowed. Her hands are flat against his chest, steadying her; with each upward drive of his fingers she flinches, and smiles sleepily. She can feel his nails, the sharpness of them. The pressure of his upturned palm on her clitoris makes her moan against her will. His fingers twist out of her, wipe a gleam across her mouth. There's always a smell like smoke to her: when he kisses the glossiness off her mouth there's a burnt taste on her lips.

He unbuckles his belt swiftly, his trousers opening at his hips. A drop of opaline fluid collects at the head of his cock. He pulls her to him, a hand gripping her back. Her underwear snagged at her knees, she cannot open her legs widely, but it's nice. He likes forcing himself between her thighs, the tangle of hair that catches him, the tuck of his balls into the valley of her legs. Sliding into her, the feeling is lushly familiar. Her smooth interior opens for him, seems created for him, takes a firm, exacting hold. His cock drives high, making her gasp and giggle; she flexes the muscles that wrap him, and he snuffles. Though there is never a moment when they aren't aware of the minutes, he will not hurry. To rush seems disrespectful. She knows he's being thoughtful, and why. He tries to be a good man, and all the time she's known him she has been stalked by the knowledge that she's damaging something rare. She glances at the grizzled sky, sees the shivering silhouette of gum leaves. No strings: *but every time she sees him, a little bit of her breaks away. She never knows what to say, so she digs her nails into his flanks and growls, 'Hurry. Hard.' Not at all what she'd wanted to say: just ugly* hurry, awful *hard.*

She's never met a man who needed to be told twice, who didn't jump like a colt turned loose. He surges into her, his fingers tangling her dress: she feels the tug and punch of him, the head of his cock striking the muscles guarding her womb. Tomorrow she will ache. Tonight, though, she puts her arms up to hold him as he comes with bitten-lip dignity, the softest of sounds escaping him. When she comes, it's a catfight; with him, there's always grace.

She's learned to be still in the first moments afterwards, that it hurts him to move or be touched. He is sometimes too bashful to look at her, so she never makes him. While he rests she runs a fingertip round the butterfly curve of his ear. She feels him subsiding bit by bit within her, and it tickles, so she laughs; eventually he laughs too, and swats her hand away. They step apart from each other, wiping their eyes, straightening their clothes. They hear the distant spillage of laughter, the popping of balloons. He plucks shards of eucalypt bark from her hair. A claggy river is meandering down her leg, and she doesn't have any tissues. A flutter in the canopy makes him look up to see a fruit bat clambering on a branch, and he points it out to her. Animals everywhere they go. She lifts her chin and watches it, completely unsurprised.

He sits in his seat, hands pressed to his face. He wishes he had sunglasses, for everything seems to unnaturally glare, a stringent, judgmental, inescapable stare levelled solely on him because surely he's caught the attention of the entire world, surely he flickers like neon. He is not generally given to melodrama, but all he can think is *I am doomed*.

He has torn her words into pieces, and then ripped them again: there must never be anything to find. Even with the story in the bin, he hadn't felt safe – he'd wished for matches, an incinerator, some bottomless pit dug kilometres from home. What he'd truly wished was that he had not destroyed it, for he wanted to read it again. He

---

had reached for the telephone, for the sound of her voice, driven to describe his torment, but stopped – it was what she wanted him to do. She's sly, a wolf in wolf's clothes: his life would be easier if he could only stop shambling into her traps. She toys with him as if he has wire for bones and stuffing for a heart. It's almost a year since he met her, that innocuous *How do you do*, and in that time she has crept from nonentity to skulker to luring sprite: now, inexplicably, she's a blazing sphere in his mind, she is all he thinks about. He has looked up her address in the directory, his fingers travelling thread-thin roads. He has rung her phone number so often that he knows it off by heart. He remembers everything she's told him, her details imprinting on him. She likes pyjamas, spending money, Easter eggs, and cakes; she has no time for hippies or cooking, for Christian names bestowed upon cars. He envies the friends she visits, the dog she walks, the people she greets in the street. When he is with her he notices the veins in her hands, the length of her lashes, the freckles dotting her arms. He wakes to her each morning, and falls asleep under her; she's the first thing he remembers, the last clear thought in his mind. Each dawn he scoops his

———

stiff cock to his body and lies in bed a few minutes longer, riding on cloudy recollections of her.

He sighs, shifts in his seat; he's cramped and over-heated, everything his gaze settles on is blinding. Were someone to stop and enquire after his health he might shriek or burst into tears. Certainly he would flee, praying there was an edge to the world after all, determined to throw himself off it.

She is beating him to death with feathers. For that's what it is, this conflagration in his mind: it is the death of something, it's doom. Even if he were to walk away now – eradicate her face, her gruffy voice, every last thing about her – it is too late, he is already changed. He has already forgotten the man he was, cannot remember what he thought about before his thoughts brimmed with her. There's a word he's heard used to describe men so smitten, a term suitably swollen with scorn: *cuntstruck*. The expression makes him bridle. That isn't how it is for him – at least, he can't believe it's that simple. She had promised *no strings*, but for him such insouciance is not possible. He cannot sleep with someone he doesn't care for, he is not a man for whom sex can mean nothing. If he were to go to her, it would mean defeat and betrayal; it would also mean that he liked her, that he'd stumbled close to loving her. Because sometimes that is what he feels – a kind of boiling-brained, skittish-handed, epileptic-hearted madness that can only be described as the teeter before the collapse. He wonders if there's any greater pleasure than this gleeful vertigo. But the very worst disaster would be to fall in love with her: better to be cuntstruck, that pubescent, passing thing.

He looks over the top of his fingers, peeks surreptitiously out the window. Nothing moves beyond the glass, nothing looks back at him – yet he can't shake the sensation of being watched, the fear that his thoughts are broadcasting. He is thirsty – he would like to hold a streaming garden hose to his face and gulp down water until he was giddy. Dry and jittery, clothed in sacking and burdened by rubble, he hasn't been comfortable in his skin since the moment she made her inelegant offer to screw him until he screamed.

It was the kind of proposal he knows men dream about. He had been stunned to hear it, every atom in him electrified; he'd felt slammed against glass. And he'd meant

———

what he said, *he would if he could*, but the point was that he could not. Nevertheless he'd taken the offer home with him, closed tightly in his hand. He had undressed without switching on the light, draping his good clothes on the arm of a chair; and only under the blankets, in blackest silence, did he open his fingers to consider what he held. Against the pitch, the words smouldered like coal. He was still an attractive man, a desirable man, a man who could, if he wanted, make himself a different man – one who kept secrets, who lived life in layers, who had stepped cavalierly off the path. Who had answered the siren call of change that is never completely quiet in his ears. The opportunity had come tantalisingly near: he wondered if he was a fool to have let it go. To have let *her* go, for he would doubtlessly never hear from her again. A fault-line had opened when he'd turned her down – she had had little more to say to him afterwards, she hadn't stayed at the party for long. He could not remember what, if anything, he had said as goodbye.

He'd lain cold on the mattress in the darkness, swallowing back the need to howl; in the morning he had woken peevish, his jaw sore with gritted teeth. His first

---

recollection was this: *she is gone*. And because he could not endure the thought of it, he had tramped through the day thinking nothing.

And now, a day later, it is as if a great rain has stopped falling, he has been rescued from a landslide, he's stepped off a ledge and discovered he can fly. Flipping through his mail he had recognised her handwriting immediately; and tearing open the envelope he'd found the tale she had written, a hymn of promises, a portrait of a future, an invitation that ran for thousands of words. He had read it over and over, the pages creasing in his hands. He saw the words clearly for what they were, a lure; he also saw things he had never seen before. The forest, the stars, the whisper. Pressing her, kissing her, coming into her. He leaned against the tree with her, thoughtless, lit inside. His blood had skipped through him, he'd crossed and recrossed his legs. He had read the words repeatedly, guarding them from view, a cradle of want and need rocking in the depth of his stomach. Sweat had broken on his lip, he'd chewed a thumbnail raggedly. He had read her words until only three words remained, each of them simple to say: *I am doomed*. He was decided.

———

He looks again out the car window, sizing up her house. As a building it is completely unremarkable, typical of its down-to-earth neighbourhood, well-kept and unpretentious, neither hovel nor mansion. A house at which nobody would look twice, the perfect place to hide something from sight. He's wretchedly nervous, desperately willing. He would gather his courage, if he had any: but he feels void of characteristics, excavated, blank. He is vacated, to be refilled.

The front yard of her house is riotous with plants: somewhere there will be a tap, a hose under which he could douse his head. He will knock on her door, request a cup of tea, make no comment on the fact that everything has become extraordinary. He steps from the car, locks it and pockets the key, crosses the empty road. He lifts the gate latch and closes it behind him, the first and last thing he will do.

The house is tidier than he expected, more sparsely decorated. Each room is painted a different, dusky shade. She owns things that people are drawn to touch and admire but he wanders around making no comment, keeps his hands to himself. She is in front of the stereo, undecided what to play. When she'd opened the front door he could tell she was astounded: she said, 'It's not fair – I'm all messy,' and frowned like he had cheated her. The threadbare jumper she's wearing has holes in the cuffs for her thumbs. She'd put the kettle on and they had sized up one another, separated by an expanse of cream tile. 'I hate you,' he had said, and she smiled. Her front teeth are ghost-grey, having died in a crash. There is nothing on her feet but a pair of striped socks, her boots left toppled outside. They had smiled and shuffled and looked at the floor, both feeling silly and amazed. While the tea brewed he drifted through the house, into the study, to the scrutiny of books. He scans the shelves for titles he's read but each word feels foreign to him. There's a maze of pictures on the dark-blue walls, none of them an image he has seen before. There is a photo in a frame on the broad brown desk, four black-and-white children standing sombrely in a row. He picks her from her siblings immediately. A prickling at his neck makes him turn to see, through the window, a great dog looking in, its paws on the sill, its eyes following him. Her Cerberus, he thinks; her hunting hound. 'I shouldn't be here,' he suggests, and the mongrel agrees.

Music rises; she comes to the door, a mug of tea wavering in each hand. She sets the mugs on the bookshelf and stands back, annoyed. The tea looks undrinkable, speckled and orange – she has never been anything of a hostess. 'Sorry,' she says, and unkempt and ashamed she has never been more beguiling, less alluring. He wants to kiss her and shake her, he wants to rewind time. He hadn't been joking when he said he hates her – he does. He

———

wishes he'd never met her. He feels corroded by her, the clean edges of his life nibbled and made septic. He does not think she's beautiful – she's not. She is punishment for some unknown, accidental, apparently unforgivable crime. He wants returned everything she's bled from him, his serenity, his balance, his trustworthiness. He wants to lie alongside her, put his lips to her breast, lick her wrists and ankles, taste the darkness between her legs. It saddens him to think he is nothing more than a man.

Her eyes are on the floating ants of tea. 'You don't have to drink it, if you don't want,' she says.

'Thank you,' he answers. 'That's a relief.' And she glances at him, and grins lopsidedly, taking it on the chin. How strange it is, that he stands here, this man who must have a real life beyond this room but who has always been, under this roof, somebody imagined. How odd that he should have taken form and stepped through her front door. She slouches, asks archly, 'So what *do* you want?'

And looking back he'll see that this was the instant when he dropped – with no final flourish, with astonishing ease – the entire weighty suit of his life: when he answers, blasé, 'I want to see the whole house.'

————

She considers him a moment, knowing what he's done. Then steps beckoningly backward, waving a hand.

The bedroom is only two strides along the hall. Of all the rooms, it is the least decorated. He crosses its threshold like a pagan into a cathedral, faintly afraid, wide-eyed. The walls are lake-blue, the carpet artery-red, the ceiling dove-white over his head. The window is open and a breeze rocks the venetian blind on its cords, tapping it lightly against the window frame. He wonders if, years from now, the clink of metal striking wood will remind him of this day.

The bed has a timber, slatted frame, pale linen and a scarlet quilt. Four pillows laze over each other, two on each side; embroidered on their cases are tiny ruby flowers. On a shelf in a corner sits a hairless stuffed toy; her slippers lie capsized beside the bed. It is a room of straight lines and primary colours, like a child's box of building-blocks. She crosses the red carpet to close the blind; then says something to him, and for some reason it's as if he has forgotten how to understand. 'No,' he says. 'I'm fine.'

She regards him through the hazy light; then sits

———

beside the pillows, pushing up her sleeves. It is warm in the room, the spring breeze is humid, but it seems right. There is something autumnal about him, he is subtle and calm, yet she has always imagined him against a background of the hottest summer nights, the most scorching afternoons. And sometimes, in her imagination, they have fallen giggling and feral into each other's arms, and sometimes it has been like this: muted, forlorn. She knows what his presence here is costing him and there's no victory in it, it doesn't make her happy.

He sits on the far edge of the bed, not touching her. 'So,' he says. 'I don't –' He frowns, starts again. 'This is not what I'm used to. I don't have practice at this.'

She says, 'I know.'

'I might – disappoint you.'

'It's not the first time you've said that.'

'But I really mean it. Today, right now, I mean it.' He laughs abjectly. 'And then – my god – you'll despise me.'

She watches his gaze shift to the floor, the flicker of his curveless lashes. She says, 'Do you think I would despise you for being human – do you think that's the kind of

———

person I am? Somebody who would laugh at you? Do you judge me that poorly?'

'No,' he answers. It's not a question of judgment. 'I don't know.'

'Do you think all these months have been about something so trivial? That everything between us is that petty, that frail?'

'I don't know,' he repeats. 'I hope not. You know what I mean.'

She shakes her head ruefully, as if she's disappointed after all. She looks at her hands, at her blunt fingernails. It is miracle enough that he's here. She says, 'I will never forget that you came to this house, you sat down in this room. I never believed you would do it. So you've already proved yourself better than I imagined.'

He almost smiles. 'And I haven't even taken off my clothes yet.'

She laughs, delighted, joyfully; she sinks against the bedhead, drawing up her knees. 'If you *were* to disappoint me,' she says, and there's suddenly a dangerous streak to her voice, a purr filtered through fangs, 'do you know what I would do?'

'I dread to think.'

'I would make you take off your shirt and undo your belt and lie down on the bed.'

He'll remember this moment later and think, *Was it too late, then, to turn back?* Had he even wanted to turn back? Through all the months that brought him here, had there ever been a minute when he was sure that what he was doing was what he wanted to do?

But in the moment itself, he doesn't think. He slips his shirt over his head, slides his belt from his trousers and lets it coil to the floor. She raps the pillows with her knuckles: 'Lie down. Face down. Shut your eyes.'

He does so, stretching out, feeling somewhat foolish. The linen beneath his bare chest is smooth and sheerly cool. He tucks his hands at his temple and closes his eyes.

Apprehension rises like vapour from him, but she ignores it. She runs her gaze over his slender back, the shoulderblades lying flat, the ripples of spine and rib. It's a finer back than she'd imagined, fluid and pared-down, without a sliver of excess. She casts an expert eye over places that, daintily handled, will make him snatch his breath and squirm. She knows how to tighten every muscle in him, she knows what feels divine or like torture. She could probe her thumb between his legs, graze his balls with the flat of her nail, and he would buck as if stung by a spark. Instead her hands flutter harmlessly down to the shallows of his ribs.

It's an instant before he even realises he is being touched. His flesh feels it before his mind does, and goose-bumps prickle his skin. Her fingers coast up his sides, down his spine, swivel like dancers across his hips. They skip and swirl so he thinks of leaves, how lightly they must fall. She twines patterns over him, knowing he is following her fingers in search of message or a meaning. She runs her fingers into his hair, loops his ears, surfs his neck. When she tickles the hollows of his waist he flinches, resisting the urge to wriggle; he holds nervously still when her fingertips crest the rise of his arse. But she doesn't trespass, she doesn't even speak: and gradually he comes to understand he is safe.

His thoughts drift.

He thinks of fish, and silver. He feels the beach, the sand, the drag of currents against him. He hears laughter

———

in a dead-end street, the thwack of leather against willow, birds calling in the morning when he walks. He hears a trammel on wooden floors, applause from many hands. He sees rooms, paths, places, trees, hears words he hasn't spoken said by voices he doesn't know. There's a benign music in his ears – guitars, cellos, piano, drums. The breeze crosses him, riffling his hair, looping through his fingers. That morning he'd dreamed of the ocean, the surface of the water clogged with sinewy seaweed. The seaweed was there for a purpose, to help him walk on waves: instead he'd dived, feeling the sun flare for a final time on the glowing soles of his feet. The water had been salty and roaring in his ears, emerald-green, studded with bubbles: it had filled his limbs and sunk him, but he hadn't been afraid. He had been understanding, even grateful, for drowning is surely the best and finest, the most forgivable way to die—

When he opens his eyes she is watching him mildly. The room seems darker, the blind knocks the window frame. She smiles, and he smiles back at her: he feels drowned and revived. Sitting up, he takes her wrists, holding her hands to the mattress. He kisses her hard, forcing his body against her. He runs a hand under her jumper and bra, closes his fingers into her breast. He feels brutal with the need to fuck her as fiercely as he can. He pulls the buttons of her jeans, yanks the denim down her legs. She chuckles with sultry pleasure, her knees knocking together. He drags her underwear off her, stern as if undressing a child. He kisses her stomach, the curls of her hair, sucks the muggy chambers of her cunt. She tastes like a cave, like subterranean water, like moths and stalactites. His body is bowed with its want to be in her, he's almost snarling. He shrugs his trousers to his knees, forces her legs further apart. He slides into her so easily, after such a long fight. She stiffens and arches against him, showing her throat. He grapples to contain himself, but each hard thrust demands just one more, another. He bites his lip, lunges, feels something inside start to run. His eyes fill with liquid and he puts his face in her shoulder and knows he is not going to win—

She lifts her knees, and the movement is distraction: he catches himself, his strewn thoughts, he feels like he's been dragged by horses. He mutters in her ear, *sorry, sorry, sorry, sorry*, until he trusts himself to move again. He

———

straightens so they can see his cock dipping in and out of her, streaked with wetness, magically shining. The sight makes her laugh, elated – he laughs too. He takes her in his arms and cuddles her, and she kisses him, still laughing, wipes his eyes with her hand. 'You are divine to me,' she tells him, and he catches her hand and kisses it, tasting the brine of his tears. In these sun-showery moments, they love one another.

She guides him onto his back and straddles him, but doesn't let him slip inside her: his penis touches the mouth of her cunt and is held there, poised, but when he tries to press himself up she grinds his wrist, and he goes still. He is sweating. She looks down at him, her hair in her eyes, her jumper rumpled and askew. She sees his chest, its scattering of hair, the twin flat disks of his nipples. She feels the anticipation in his body and in her own, the twanging of every nerve. She could stay like this forever, but the moment is never allowed to last: when she sinks darkly onto him, his cock is forced deep and high, drawing from her a buried moan. She pulls off her jumper and bra and crouches on him naked, a bent-kneed, blue-eyed, bare-foot demon. Her muscles flex around his cock, rocking him a little. He runs his hands over her breasts as she rises and falls on him. Lulled by the steady rhythm, he closes his eyes and wonders *Who am I*.

And while he isn't looking she drops a hand between his thighs and buries her fingers into the sensitive clenching of his balls. He jumps awake, swearing, says, 'Do that again.' She does, and he feels radiance; then shakes his head stubbornly when she says, 'Sit up.'

'No –'

She tightens her jaw, amused that someone so vulnerable could also be so bold. She huddles nearer to murmur in his ear. 'We might never meet again, and I want you to sit up.'

She slips from him and turns away: on hands and knees, she's sturdy. He brushes a hand over her arse, swipes a knuckle up her soaked cunt. He settles behind her and lets her wait a punishing moment, not touching, not speaking, before gliding into her. Now it's she who swears. He holds her steady with an arm under her breasts and drives with authority against her: as soon as he feels her change of pace, the throb of fluid, he lets himself come. His nails rip her, his body opens out. For a second he

———

thinks the surging within him won't stop, that he will pulse for days.

They sag on the mattress, breathing hoarsely. She gazes glassily at the open door, at upturned pictures on the walls. Her heart is thudding – another beat inside keeps time. The venetian blind knocks metallically; from the loungeroom, the music still plays. She holds a hand in front of her, and it is shaking.

She looks at him – he knows it, but doesn't look at her. He would kiss her if it wouldn't make him seem thankful, or pleased with himself. His hands spanned like stars across his chest, he recollects how it felt to go down to the sea.

———

She works in the garden for the first time in a week. It's like catching up with an old friend. She has always felt the pull of the earth, loved spilling life's green blood. Spring is her favourite season, with its luminous lime growth and freshness: everything is woken and spirited, everything races toward the sun. She has not yet brought him out here, to this large paling-fenced Eden where she is no artist's idea of Eve, but there's no particular reason why. One day, if they had time, she would pour some water and follow him out here and she'd introduce him to the plants, tell him their stories – there's a past and a future, a grand scheme for each one. It would bore him, probably. He never speaks of a garden. She suspects she's always, in

———

everything, a little boring to him – she sees his sights drift dully and there's nothing she can say, no topic she can think of that will repair the damage done. All, so far, they've found in common are restlessness and a liking for animals; sweet-toothedness, bitten fingernails, and a sense of the absurd. It's quite a long list, really.

She wipes her face with her t-shirt, leans against the spade. She is aware of being watched by a cat like a caracal, a drowsy wolf-dog. Birds are also watching, waiting for her to overturn a creature that, dazzled by the abrupt bright, will not see the swooping shadow, will not sense oncoming wings. There are canvas gloves on her hands but crumbs of dirt have worked their way past the cuffs and disintegrated inside the fingers, annoying her. She shakes the gloves off, throws them aside. She's not afraid of spiders or creeping, crawling things. She is not afraid of being bitten. She thinks there is nothing that really makes her scared. It is nice to think that such indifference is courage, but it could be that she simply doesn't care.

When he is here, he trembles. He knows his way around the house but he is still determinedly an outsider, a tangle of exposed nerves, his neck noosed by hesitation and dread. He sits uncomfortable as a virgin on the couch, looks about with flighty despair. He is on a rack of guilt, and when she crouches close to him she can almost hear him screaming. *I want to screw you till you scream.* It is infinitely endearing, his battle between daring and dismay. Yet she knows, too, that fear rubs shoulders with hatred, and she wonders what he's thinking when she kisses him, what he ponders on the long journey away from here.

It is a cool day, this afternoon in early spring. A gust bowls over the empty plant pots, shudders the near-naked branches of the apricot and apple trees. She picks from the hole she's digging a morsel of blue porcelain, a bite of a long-lost plate. She loves to unearth things, bones and coins, plastic baubles from childhoods past. She drops the fragment of china into the pocket of her trousers, dusts her hand on her clothes.

Nonetheless she's learning that it's useless trying to guess what he thinks. She rarely gets it right. He is elusive and changeable – she is conscious of trying to read a language she doesn't fully understand, of searching for a regular beat in an eccentric tune. She has always thought herself a good judge of character, yet she can rarely predict with certainty anything about him. She will do or say something and be sure that, once again, she's managed to spoil everything with her bovine, ludicrous ways – only to find that he won't have flinched, he'll hardly even have noticed. Other things, often small things, seem to grind into him, alarm him and raise his voice until she murmurs *shh*, *shh*. He is only calm on the outside, maybe; inside, he's like the breeze. He follows fewer rules than she does, and she follows almost none. She coughs and smiles, wipes her cheeks with her palm. He is proving himself nothing if not surprising.

One of the surprises is this: his perfect skin. He's like a painting, like silk. He's unmarred, as if nothing has ever harmed him; the hair on his arms glints tawny in the light. It makes her aware of her rough hands, her scuffed knees, the windburn that weathers her lips. The bed does not seem sufficiently gentle to hold him – face, chest, arms, feet, like *feathers*; hands like hummingbird wings. Such fineness makes her feel pagan: she'd like to bite him, scratch him, tie him up, vandalise him. When she thinks about him in the mornings, she holds him down, carves in her nails, kisses him so hard it splits his lip and makes him

———

bleed. Sinks in her fangs, makes him plead. Dawn is the time he comes to her willingly, when there's nothing to which he must return, she can do with him whatever she wants. A hundred rooms, a hundred scenarios, everything done that she can't do in real life, all this while he's walking the bank of a river like some hungry, saintly aesthete.

A grey bird – a wattlebird – lands on the fence, glaring like wire at her. She turns her back to it, hefting the spade. A spade is a cutting tool; a shovel is for lifting or moving. She knows this, has known it for years, can't remember where she learned it. Mostly she is self-taught: she has learned how to grow things by watching things grow. This ground has not been dug for decades, and the blade makes a deep, clean incision.

When she was younger, without a home of her own, she made a sport and a habit of fucking outdoors, collecting remarkable locations like a connoisseur. The Exhibition Building gardens at midnight, drunk on pink champagne. The sandpit of a state school at her best friend's twenty-first. A beach in Venice, where an old man paused to watch and mumbled something in Italian. The top deck of a towering playground rocket – later she discovered she could see

———

the playground from the window of her train, and the sight of that rocket standing so stiff and proud always made her wryly smile. Not one of her outdoor settings had been comfortable, not one was worth revisiting, yet she's ridiculously fond of the memories. She puts her boot to the spade, feels the twang of snapping roots. 'Well, maybe the rocket,' she says. The cat looks away, closing golden eyes.

It's not what she wants for him, though – nowhere inhospitable for that pristine skin. With him, she would like to lie naked in a safe and silent bed, her knees drawn up, her body tucked to his; and fall asleep with his arm between her breasts, his heart near to her, his breath brushing her shoulder. In the ebony marrow of night he could slip inside her, hardly rousing her from sleep, and rock her as gently as water; she would not speak but would close her hand in his, and it would just be him and her and the dark and the bed and the solidness of him against her, the sleek pressure of him within. He'd roll her onto her back and kiss her throat quietly until he came, and he would sleep then like a kitten in the sheltered crook of her arm—

She pinches her lip, staring down at the grass. The sun

---

has burned through the clouds and she feels it on the back of her arms. The cat and dog watch her drive the spade into the dirt and leave it wedged there, wavering. She sits in the shade of the apple tree, shielding her face with her hands. It's a mistake to imagine such things about him, an injurious mistake.

In a few days he is going away – his work puts him on planes and flies him to subdued cities, soundless countries, up and out of her reach. Everything could change in his absence, she knows. Far away, he might see her for what she is, a paper doll; she might wane like a ripple on water. He might fly home full of words like a wasteland, speaking in a voice that sheds fog. Or he will miss her, she doesn't know.

She sits in the garden under the bony branches of the apple tree, her shadow pooled beneath her, her hands across her eyes.

———

There are things they'll never tell each other. Their lives have a core of not-telling – they bite their tongues, lower their eyes, feign indifference in public every day – but there are also things they won't say to one another. There's some pleasure in this being so. Everything they do, they must do in darkness – even in broad daylight, they're forced to live in the shade. So it's nice to keep things light and airy between them, to laugh and talk about things of no consequence, to tickle his feet rather than philosophise. She tells him she missed him, when he was away, but only a tiny bit, not very much: he answers that he had a splendid journey, he's sorry he had to come home.

Today it is his birthday: he feels young and not quite

———

tame. He lies on his back in the scraggly grass of her yard, eating oranges he bought in a netting bag. She lies beside him, her fingers hooked behind her head, looking up at the sky. She says, 'You know how you're supposed to see things in clouds – faces and trucks and saucepans and things? I never see stuff like that. All I see is clouds.'

'That's because you've got no imagination,' he tells her. 'Look there – that one looks like a lion standing on one of those barrels at a circus.'

She frowns at the bulk-headed clouds, whines, 'I can't see it – where?'

'Nowhere,' he says. 'I made it up.'

She watches from the corner of an eye as he giggles to himself; an orange has left a spark of its juice on his lips. 'You're not funny,' she says.

'Yes I am,' he answers, with the confidence that is always there when he refutes some claim she's made. Sometimes he reminds her of a bird – a gossamer thing shot through with certainty, softness wrapped round an iron will. She looks away from him, to the clouds. He nips strands of pulp from the fruit peel, still chortling to himself; then tosses the skin into the grass and says, 'More.'

———

'Get it yourself. You know where they are.'

'But it's my *birthday* . . .'

She sighs heavily, gets to her feet.

'A good one. Not squashy. Firm, but not too firm. Just right.'

She glances back at him, wonders if she's a bad influence on him. When she opens the bag the oranges tumble from it and roll away impetuously, opulently bright against the green grass.

'No bruises,' he adds.

'I'm taking no notice of you,' she says.

He smiles, closing his eyes against the sky. He knows she will find for him the finest fruit that's there; she knows he is an uncomplaining man, unfussy, that he'll be happy with what he gets. She guesses he has always been this way – she sees the slight boy he might have been, a child of simple pleasures who didn't feel a need for new things, for envy, for achievements over which to brag. She wishes she had known him when he was twenty years old and learning to feel his way through the world. She cannot decide if they would have been friends, had they met at that age.

Her shadow mutes the colours blooming behind his

eyelids. His hand glides up her leg, over ankle and calf and knee and thigh, finding its way below the blowsy white skirt she wears only as a treat for him, because it is his birthday. His fingers slither through the slipperiness of her, snuggle into the bed of her cunt. He smiles, but doesn't open his eyes. On this dry sunny day, the earth feels tender beneath him, and seems to lazily spin. He remembers coming home drunk when he was still a kid, a teenager, barely old enough to be allowed in the bar – he'd lain sweating while his bedroom spun hideous cartwheels until he had wanted to die. He'd dragged himself to his feet and lurched to the bathroom, seasick with nausea. He had stretched out groaning on the cold tiled floor and his mother had found him there, her favourite child, and she'd laughed, not angry, but with such love and pity for him. She had put her hand against his face and he remembers the feeling still, years later: the peaceful touch of her.

She reaches out the hand that doesn't hold the orange, and gently touches his face. She hovers above his hip-bones, balanced on bent legs. He smells the sweetness of fruit on her fingers, the citrus bite to her breath. He should open his eyes but he doesn't, and he doesn't want to. The

———

fruit is a small weight that she places on his chest, in the seam where his ribs arch to his heart. She undoes his jeans and shuffles them down his thighs so he feels a cat's-paw of breeze glide across his stomach and draw like thread around his lifting cock. He hears the splicing calls of birds, the bony knock of eucalypt leaves, the mystery cracklings in the grass. There's grass tied around his fingers, holding him down. He hears the familiar hitch of her breath as he goes into her, feels the jolt of her spine when he strikes muscle. She is the slickest creature he's ever known; her cunt is a place created for him, made to take him exactly. She rocks her arse, her skirt bunching beneath her: the tug on his cock is unbearably pleasant, making him afraid to breathe. She rolls the orange around his stomach, watches it drop to the grass and trundle away, then hunches forward to whisper against his brown throat. 'You're beautiful,' she tells him. He feels like he's heard it all his life. She sits back, sinking him, easing from him, bearing down again. He raises a hand and his fingers forge a path underneath the rucked cloth of her skirt. He pushes his fingers amongst the niches of her cunt, tweaks the hard hiding bead. She yelps like she's hurt but he knows her

———

well, and does not pause. His fingers exploring, he feels himself, the taut flank of his penis gliding against his own knuckle. He slots a finger inside her to feel his cock working in her, and smiles to think he's intruding on something that wants privacy. He applies two fingertips to her clit and rubs it rushingly. Her head hanging, her hands on her thighs, she rams herself down on him forcefully: when she comes it's without caring that they are outdoors, where anyone nearby could hear. It's sort of sexy, it makes him laugh – then suddenly makes him come, his arms enclosing her, her ribcage embraced to his own. He loves to hold her; she loves to be held. He comes high into her and for a moment he is there too, swirling fluidly through her. He imagines himself and his come spreading like a starburst inside her, racing to catch hold.

She sits back panting, wiping moisture from her lip. He opens and shuts his eyes against the brilliance of the sky. He feels the burden of secretions pushing him down until his cock nestles in a lightless copse of hair and soaking flesh. His arms draping away from her, his fingers close around a wayward orange. He holds up the fruit but she shakes her head and sighs, 'No, no.'

So he peels the orange and eats it himself, lying in the grass on a vivid afternoon with blackbirds flying by, his fingers as pungent as orchards and bushfire. She lies sleepily at his side, examining the clouds for something she can recognise; he travels on inside her, spinning slowly in the dark.

When he is gone she finds on the floor a hair curled as intricately as a treble clef. She sits on the tiles with her back to the wall and the fine strand rests in her palm, shifting minutely in a current she cannot feel, perhaps the draught of her breathing or the beat of her heart or the pump of blood under skin. The hair is fawn, the colour of him; it twists like a knot unfurling, trembling and tilting on her palm. She remembers how he used to tremble when he came here. He doesn't do that much anymore. The house is familiar to him now – both of them fancy that the house is actually fond of him – and he's familiar with her and the black road that brings him here, he knows what's in the cupboards, he'll pour himself some water, he knows

———

how tightly to turn off the taps. He will walk through the rooms unaccompanied, there's nothing much shy about him now. Only this stray hair shivers.

Today he had gone into the study without her, to cast his eye over her library. She wonders if he remembers that the study was the first room he went to alone. This after-noon she had watched, inexplicably nervous, as he scanned the spines without comment. He has never been one to keep his opinions to himself – if he sees something critical, he'll criticise. And her collection is not rag-tag, she is particular, keeping only those books that she loves or have meaning, callously tossing all others in the bin. If he slandered one of them she would feel her affection for it falter, there would be a small death in the room. But he had said nothing, had raised a hand and touched an orna-ment with a finger, had glanced sideways and smiled at her.

She had smiled back at this man who knows her, the place of her, the interior of her, but who sometimes, of late, has seemed a stranger to her, someone growing more distant with each nearer step he takes. She watches him through a kaleidoscope coloured by the peculiar

———

shades of their past, remembering where he came from, where he believes he belongs. She senses he has recently come to conclusions, and that his decisions will soon exclude her. It has made him feel guilty – thus withdrawn and sullen, thus coolly resentful. Maybe he resents, too, the very thing he's decided upon: a future he can envisage all the way to the end. It is probably not how he wanted his life to be – like a book already written – worse, already read.

Or maybe she is simply imagining it: alone, she's sometimes stalked by monsters of doubt. It's difficult to decide what's justified, what's simply the sour offspring of the situation. Destabilised by love for him, her life is rudderless, she's lost her sense of proportion; but she hopes she'll have sense enough not to protest, to concede without demeaning argument when he comes to her, gaunt and tired, wanting to be free.

He had taken her hand in his own. 'Come on,' he said. 'There isn't much time.'

But she hadn't moved and he had looked at her and for an instant the old gentleness was there again, the hard-eyed stranger brought down. She'd drawn him to her, guided his hand down the loose front of her jeans, felt his fingers push inside her, gripped his shirt to keep steady. She's always drenched by the mere thought of him – even at that moment, feeling trampled and uncertain, she'd been wet as a seal. She had once feared he would despise her for it, this slavish devotion that greets him every time. It was probably a stupid concern.

She had unzipped her jeans and let them crumple to her calves, stepped out of them with a shake of each foot. 'Tell me,' she'd said, 'about the first time you fucked a girl.'

He smiled cleverly, looking into her eyes, his fingers rocking like boats. 'Well, you know, it was a long time ago. I was very young. Even when I was merely a boy, women wanted me.'

'Of course.'

'I was eight years old, maybe ten.' He smoothed her underwear to her knees, touching a fleet kiss to her arse. 'She was a wild-headed vixen, eighteen or thereabouts, a slattern from the nearby village.'

'How very Byronic,' she'd mused.

'I remember that she could never quite contain her cushiony breasts inside her buttonless shirt, that she smelt

———

of cheese and briar and whisky swigged from tankards at the alehouse.'

She had giggled into his chest, bumping her forehead against him. She'd undone his belt and his trousers had dropped, ballasted by coins and the trifles he collects. She has always liked the unveiling of his underwear, discovering the styles and the colours he prefers. The clothes he wears are, for her, a glimpse over the wall of his world. 'So what happened?' she asked. 'Tell me everything.'

He had taken her elbows and turned her to the window, away from the flat-faced judgment of the novelists, away from himself. They'd gone down as if in prayer. The carpet was coarse, their shins would burn. 'She was a poxy slut employed as a serving girl. She carted water from the well, darned socks, mopped the floors. She came to me in the middle of the night. She wanted to make a man of me.'

'How wonderful.' His fingers were weaving through the maze of her cunt, stroking the groove of her buttocks, icing her arsehole with fluid. His chest at her shoulderblades, she could feel the nearness of his cock, the waft of heated impatience. 'Go on.'

———

'I was inexperienced, as you can imagine.' His fingers were linked by glossy strands that stretched like a sea creature. He pulled her close suddenly, pushed a finger into her arse, took her shudder into himself. 'Nonetheless, it all came naturally. I rose to the occasion, I think.'

Every atom in her was swimming, disrupted, she couldn't concentrate her thoughts. He painted her skin with cream scooped from within her, drove his thumbs deep inside her, eased her tense muscles apart. It hurt a little; it didn't. Distracted, breathing shallowly, she couldn't remember what to ask next. He was leaning against her, his cock slightly touching her. 'Careful,' she had muttered. 'Slowly.'

'I bounced on her like she was a trampoline, that filthy wench,' he sighed. He was on his haunches, very still. She backed against him, felt the resistance of her anus and the looping stalwart muscles there – then the puncturing as he pushed into her, the spiked intake of his breath. Her spine arched around him, her fists clenched on the floor, she remembered instantly the sensation, like speed, unpleasantly divine. He sank his fingers in her hips, his teeth bit his lip. His cock felt blinded, enveloped in plush inkness – he thought of velvet curtains plunging down on an ancient stage. He felt the stranglehold of her arse around him as he drew his cock in and out, moving with the gravest care, each hindered slide into her reminding him anew of the smothering curtains, the airlessness of them. He had closed his eyes, felt feathers against his shoulders, water across his face. He had fallen into velvet, a depthless vat of suffocating scarlet that would kill him lovingly and without pain so he would never know the exact moment when he died—

'Come to me,' she'd said.

It frightened him a little, this new place in her, this secret room of royal colours, the rules he did not understand. Each upward thrust toward her spine felt, to him, like a vampire's strike, an angel skewering his heart, the hit of a drug he couldn't live without. *Come to me* she said, and he'd come without wanting to, unstoppably as if she'd forced him to, the tunnel of her arse gripping him so ardently that for a moment he had struggled for air, had felt a leaden compression squeezing his lungs. He hardly felt her rub the sweat from his forehead and settle into his arms; they had sagged together like junkies, each holding up the other and blinking thoughtlessly at the walls, soundlessly tracing the freshly-hewn edges of their lives.

She hopes that, when everything is over, he will never forget those sweet minutes when, exhausted, they would rest in each other's arms.

'Tell me your story.' He had spoken finally. 'Tell me how you lost your virginity.'

'It was nothing,' she said.

'Nothing special, you mean?'

'No. It was exactly as you imagine.'

'I'm glad,' he'd said.

In her palm lies the day's last trace of him, this lost hair like a fleur-de-lis. She runs the hair along the top of her lip, a trick her mother taught her. A person who is alive and well will flinch at a tickle across the upper lip. A person who is unconscious, dying, will almost never react. She runs the hair back and forth on her skin, pondering. There's a storm coming tonight – she sees sable clouds massing beyond the bathroom window. Clouds like tanks, he had called them, as she'd stood by his car door, saying goodbye. A strange world he lives in, where tanks could be disguised as clouds.

She rubs her lip furiously, unable to endure the twee sensation anymore. Still alive and well, it seems.

———

They give each other an early Christmas present of questions answered with truth. He lifts her onto a table and gets down on his knees. He has already unwrapped her, slung her shorts and sandals across the room. It's a blazing hot day, cloudless and gusting, the blinds drawn down on the big windows. The north wind incites the garden shrubs to scratch against the glass. 'Let's see what I've got myself into,' he says, parting her knees. Her cunt is almost level with his gaze – he angles her slightly and then he can see every bit of her. She has trimmed her pubic hair hard, so the strands mat over her skin but are too short to catch between his fingers. A bootcamp of a haircut, he thinks; she's soldierly.

———

She's thinking of a question, her fingers clamped round the edge of the table. 'Are you happy?' she asks. 'Sometimes I think that you aren't.'

'Sometimes I'm not,' he says. Her spread thighs funnel his gaze toward their meeting point. Her vulva, undisturbed, is divided into three parts. He knows their scientific names from lessons giggled through at school, from guilty afternoons spent poring over pictures in his boyhood bedroom. He remembers how startling it was to discover the difference between the illustrations and the subject in the flesh – the unexpected textures, the unmentioned chthonic smell. Different, yet distinguishable: he can label every piece of her. Her twin flanking labial flaps are impossibly, almost outlandishly soft to his touch. He often thinks of darkness, when he thinks of this centre of her; but here, in this still room on a windy afternoon, he sees no shadows, nothing plotting or cagey. When he parts the flaps with his fingers, it's pinkness that meets his eye. The colour of a girl. He glances at her; she's waiting. 'How could I be happy all the time? It's not possible. I feel guilty. I feel ashamed. But it's not you who makes me feel those things. Don't ever think that. You fill me with a kind of . . . elation.'

'I would not like you,' she replies, 'if you didn't care enough to be unhappy sometimes.'

Spreading her labia reveals the scrap-end of flesh whose tip, pointed as a dunce's cap, juts at the top of her cunt: the labia minora, a fragment of runched skin as alien as a creature in a crashed flying saucer. Surrounded by blushing birdskin, networked by blue veins, the minora yawn to expose the mauve eye of her clitoris staring fixedly at him. Below this is the knob of her urethral opening; then a vestibule of peachy flesh, quite solid to the touch, rounded as toes or, he thinks, as a foetus hugging itself. He uses a fingertip to tug down the elastic skin of her fourchette, and glimpses the flattened entrance of her vagina. A leak of sap, almost clear, almost white, is coming from her, lubricating her many departments, sticking to his fingers. The leak is severe, yet nothing drips from her – her homemade emollient returns to her, slinks between her layers and vanishes, oozes when he touches her firmly. Not a droplet has smudged the table. He leans in, puts his face in her vulva and sniffs, smells the soap she's used struggling to mask the scent of her that is stunningly strong this close, undetectable when he sits back on his haunches. He does not take his hands or eyes off her when he says, 'Every day I wake up and I'm just so . . . excited. I climb out of bed and my feet don't touch the ground.'

She laughs, her feet swing. He closes her flaps, pats them down neatly, parts them again. Little doors.

'I walk with this ridiculous swagger,' he tells her. He traces a finger down the brown skin of her perineum to the small slit of her anus; she squirms. It's nothing, this tiny pucker, this coy button, this outsider. Her razor has missed a few downy hairs here that lie flat to her skin, sweep toward her buttocks. He wants to lay his cheek against her cunt, imagines there'd be a kind of rockpool suction, that he'd be drawn inside her as effortlessly as her syrup drains into her. He could climb her like a rockface, skate her like a lake. He uses his fingers to open her vagina, marvels at its willingness. He can see her ruddy interior, it's a sort of miracle. 'I want to tell everyone about you,' he says, gazing into her. 'Complete strangers, when I'm buying a newspaper or waiting to cross the road. *There's this girl, let me tell you.* I keep dropping your name into conversations when you've got nothing to do with it. I can hardly be bothered eating, it's just a pest of a thing. I don't want to sleep, because that's time I'm not thinking of you. I never dream about you – maybe because you are like a dream. I can't imagine you doing ordinary things, talking and walking around when I'm not here. I want you to be a doll, whose life freezes when I turn my back. But I also want you to be alive, running everywhere in the world. Living this free, cheerful life. I want you to be like a bird that perches outside my window and looks in at me with beady eyes – a bird that might fly away at any moment, never to return. I feel . . . as if I've found something that everyone in history has been trying to find. I feel like I've won millions and millions of dollars. I feel as if I'm fifteen years old. I'm as happy as an idiot. Because of you.'

She looks down at him in amazement, her head dropped to one side; she's never heard so many words spill from him. She speaks quietly, the wind outside louder than her voice so they hear the gale blowing something tinny down the road. 'I feel as if I've found whatever I've been searching for my whole life. As if I know an answer now, and the answer means I can do anything. It's . . . a happy ending.'

'We are just starting.' He lifts his eyes. 'Not ending.'

———

'Are we?'

He takes his hands and places them over her cunt, one on top of the other. He has broad palms, rangy fingers, he could nurse her whole vulva in a single hand, shut both palms over it like a pair of church gates. He knows he shouldn't have said the words, they were foolhardy, promising everything he has no right to promise, but he doesn't want to take them back. 'I hope we are,' he says. 'Who knows what will happen? There's nothing certain about my life anymore. You are in it, in me. I tell lies, and all I think about is you. I'm the same on the outside, but inside I feel as if no one knows me now. I've become this stranger to everyone, but I'm always pretending that I'm the same as I used to be. The only person I don't feel strange around is you. You and I – it could all end now – it might be that we never see the end coming, that it leaps out and grabs us when we're not expecting it, when we don't want it, that it drags us apart, and that will be terrible – I can't imagine how I'd survive it. Or maybe you'll just tire of me one day, and tell me not to come here anymore. Whatever happens, I hope it happens a long time from now. I don't want you gone. I don't want to give you up.'

———

'. . . Do you want to keep me forever?'

'I want to, yes. But I don't know how I can.' Her minora are russet, the shape of a quill, and very wet, and when he rubs them between his thumb and forefinger he's impressed by their substance – they look fragile, almost vintage, but they pluck themselves from his fingers disdainfully, dodging from his touch. He smiles, likes it, there's something so headstrong about them. The more he disturbs them, the more her odour fills the big room – an aroma that carries its own taste, which settles on his lips and at the back of his throat. He wipes her legs, runs his hands to her ankles and up again. He forages her cunt, kisses it, sits down on his heels. 'This wasn't supposed to happen,' he sighs. 'This is not the sort of thing I can take lightly. No matter what happens, you are in my heart now. I don't know how I'll get you out.'

Her eyes are shut, her head low. 'Something might change,' she says. 'You might start to hate me. I'm told that's what happens in things like this – you'll come to blame me, and then you'll despise me.'

'No,' he says, 'that's just stupid. I will never despise you. I love you, you know.'

———

She opens her eyes and looks at him. 'Did you say you love me?' she asks.

'Yes,' he says. 'Sorry.'

'It doesn't matter,' she answers. 'I love you too. From the moment I met you, I knew I would love you. I knew it – still, it seems funny that it was true. Funny, to have guessed right.'

He smiles. 'This is a good Christmas present.'

They look at each other, both growing a little red in the cheeks; she winks, and he laughs, buries his face between her legs so he doesn't have to see her. It's impossibly hot in the apex of her thighs, incredibly pungent with the odour that seems to invade his skin and wrap his bones, pull him forward, clear his mind of everything except the want to eat her cunt out of her, gobble her up messily and completely, fuck her not forcibly but nevertheless with authority, with a right to be where he is. He puffs warm air against her, his tongue making long strokes up her uneven length; he weevils into the crannies at her arsehole, cruises the bulges of her labia, nuzzles at the peak where her flaps meet in the shape of a cathedral window. Again and again his tongue makes this journey over her terrain, licking up her fluid, pressing it out of her, varnishing her with saliva, sucking it away. His hand comes up and he paws at her, tweaking and compressing, slotting into her and out again slowly at first, then rapidly, a drill. Her clitoris feels tumescent, ready to burst – he sucks and nips it, licks it repeatedly, pushes his tongue underneath it and into her frenulum, holds her ankles to still her jumping legs. He buries his nose into her, his chin. He's thinking nothing – not of the hard floor at his knees, not of the sweat between his shoulders or the smell and incomparable taste of her – he cannot think, his brain has shut down, he is nothing but lips teeth gums fingers, shrewd tongue, air heaving from lungs. He is good at doing this; she loves him doing it to her. As her climax starts to hulk in her she starts saying *No no no no*, and he answers into her cunt, *Yes, come on—*

She throws herself backward on the table, her feet kicking his chest; she comes into his face and mouth, her cunt jerking and gaping, an ugly ocean-floor crawler of a thing, a hideous delight. In a minute or two he'll go into her and she will be lovely, liquid, pliable, she'll melt on him. For now he lays his head on her pelvis, her hair bristling against

———

his cheek. She is breathing torridly, her legs jolting with shock. Her arms are splayed across the table, her fingers grappling the edge. His own hands lie calmly between her breasts. He can feel her heart galloping.

Gradually she opens her eyes. Everything she sees seems altered. *I love you.* The afternoon sun has thrown stripes from the venetian blinds to the walls. The wind-tossed shrubs are battering at the windows, making high-pitched complaint. It is nice, the way her feet hang in space; nice, the weight of his head on her stomach. *I love you.* Before she lets him into her, she will take the jug of cold water from the fridge and rinse herself with it: on this arid day, in these fainting moments, she wants to be icy for him. For now she lies without moving, knowing the table-top has gripped her damp skin and that sitting up will sting. Eventually she says, 'You haven't asked me a question.'

He looks up, past her bellybutton and breasts, his chin pressing into her stomach. 'I don't want to ask you anything.'

'Well, you have to – it's a Christmas present.'

He thinks reluctantly, the breeze of his breathing

---

coasting over her chest. He asks, 'What's the worst thing I could do to you?'

'Betray me.' She answers immediately. 'Say that you love me, but behave as though you don't.'

'Is that betrayal?'

'. . . It's the worst of betrayals, isn't it?'

Her stomach is a harmonious place to lay his head – warm; beating internally; a place to blissfully fall asleep. She is running her hands through his hair, over his eyes, around his wrists and elbows. 'Then I won't ever do that,' he promises. 'That's your Christmas present, from me to you. I promise I will never tell you I love you, but act as if I don't.'

When she chuckles, he feels the tug of it in her stomach. It strikes him as ungrateful, that she would laugh at the words. 'Thank you,' she says. 'That's the best present ever.'

It is months before they spend a night together, which would be absurd in any other situation but their own – it's summer, and when it rains there is a burnt smell that rises from the road. They're in a city that isn't their own, invited to be here as junket-guests, her keep earned by talking about herself, his keep earned by listening. He is feeling jaunty on this first afternoon, has so far had a good day. The small details that make her hotel room different from his own seem brightly fascinating. He opens the refrigerator, spins the dial of the safe, examines the charming bathroom tray of shampoo, conditioner, body lotion. 'You get a sewing kit,' he says, and he can hear the lilt of protest in his voice, as if he would ever want or envy a

———

simple cardboard sewing kit with a button and needle and a scrap of cotton tangled inside. She calls back that he can have it if he wants but he puts it down carefully, appalled at himself. It's doubtlessly handy to own such a thing, but you wouldn't want to covet it. Still, the bathroom is good; the whole room is undeniably suitable and good. It has thick green carpet and maybe thicker walls. It has a hefty peepholed door that closed with a reassuring thud. It has that mint hotel-room perfume that says *nothing lasts: all is transitory*. All fine and proper, the best he'd imagined it could be – yet he's nervous. They have waited months for this night but he's lingering, frowning, in the bathroom, the kind of thing he did as a teenager, trying to convince his reflection to confront the world on his behalf. Make the mistakes, take the blame. There's been no-going-back for months now, yet spending a night together seems to grab at his heels, commit him to something, sign his name on some dotted line.

She is lying on the bed, her hands under her head. It has been a long day for her – she looks tired, isolated. She's watching the television and doesn't glance at him: she says, 'Sometimes I see these anguished characters on

TV and I think, *They've got nothing to worry about.* Do you do that?'

'All the time.' He sits beside her, draws her to him like a small animal, puts her head in his lap and his arms around her, tenderly, fatherly – at such times he can't imagine doing anything except tucking her into bed. At such times she's sexless, childish, undesirable. Then her hand ducks between his thighs and his back stiffens, his breathing stills at the kneading of her palm against his cock, the probe and flicker of her thumb. She is wounded when he speaks of all the men there have been and might yet be in her life, but when her hands dance on him he can't help but think she's artful, she knows what is what.

She keeps her gaze on the television screen, asks, 'What do you worry about?'

'You know.' It is one of their time-worn topics.

'Are you worried now?'

Her fingers arch and ferret. It makes it difficult to locate words. 'I'm always worried.' She traces and nudges and outlines, he feels the push of his blood.

'It makes me sad, you know.'

'I know.' He answers from behind closed eyes; he

doesn't, at this moment, really care. Her fingers lift his balls and squeeze them gently and it's like a waterfall plunges down his spine, like part of him washes away. 'Stop talking,' he says. 'You talk too much.'

She laughs like a cat, looking up through messy hair. He suddenly realises this safeness about her – that she'll always laugh, that she coddles no resentment, that she's infinitely forgiving of him – as if he doesn't matter to her, or matters more than anything. Around her he needn't be anything better than a man inside a skin: not smart, not serious, not thoughtful, not domestic. There's no dust to sweep, no bills to pay, nothing broken or disrupted or disputed, nothing extraordinary made ordinary by passing years. Suddenly, in this hotel room, he sees the appeal of what he's been doing with a clarity he's not known before. With her he is newborn, a caveman, an Adam. Eat, screw, sleep, that's all: life basic as an animal's. 'I'm hungry,' he sighs. 'I want to fuck you.'

She gives him the cat-laugh, a knowing snicker as if nothing he says or does is news to her. She puts a hand on his chest and pushes him back so the mattress comes up to meet him, and as she unbuckles his jeans and slides his

———

clothes from his limbs he lies smiling at the stippled ceiling, his head empty of thought, the bed's rich quilt corrugating under his hands. She slides her mouth down his hardened cock and he feels the curve of her throat, the roof of her mouth, the muscular press of her tongue. His cock is tidy, a simple design, paler than the rest of him; neither clumsy nor trifling, there's nothing immoderate about it, it's as decorous as a penis can be. Her mouth compresses around it, her lips gripping him; the edge of her teeth, sharp as stone, razor across the thin fine skin as she sucks on him. He feels the pull of her, a primitive dragging within; he puts his hands on the crown of her head to keep her there. He does not see her hand come up but he feels, deliciously, the scratch of her nails over his testicles, the shunt of her knuckles against his arse. Her tongue ripples around him and his cock is drenched, thick and hotly soaked; she sucks him vehemently, the fleshy walls of her mouth clamping him close as any cunt. Her fingers splay across his balls, tying in his hair; she slathers him with moisture and suctions it away; saturates him swampily, licks him vigorously dry. He thinks of a leopard, the barbed roughness of tongue, the knife-like spangle of fangs. Her shoulders shudder as she drives him into her mouth, the head of his cock punching the crest of her throat. Her tongue invades the small hole in his cock's head, pokes and prods there, threatens to part him wide. She traps him against the roof of her mouth and the force of her pull makes him feel flayed, starts a tremor moving through him like a running jaguar, a harpoon of violent pleasure that makes him whimper and vaguely panic, he doesn't know what to do. She might not want this, he doesn't know; he has a certain sense that it's impolite. But she, as always, knows what she wants: she closes her hands around the root of his cock and sucks him tightly as he comes, pulsing and pushing and bucking against her teeth; then licks him placidly as he blinks at the wall, his cheeks blushing rosy. His hands and feet flinch as if recalling something forgotten. She sits up on her elbows, examining him; his face is saintly and young. She bends down and kisses him, and there's such wetness on her lips and chin: he captures her and cuddles her until he feels the concaving of her ribs. He smells the shampoo in her hair, the sea-sand scent of himself when she yelps. She wriggles out of his clutches, drops off the side of the bed and stays there, slumped on the floor. She smears her mouth with the back of a wrist, swallows the taste of him. The mushroom smell of his come fills her nose and maybe the room. 'Guess what?' she says, after a time. 'I'm hungry.'

Toward morning of their first night spent with one another, he steps out of bed and goes to the bathroom. He knows she sleeps lightly but he is soundless on narrow feet and racing-green carpet. He shuts the bathroom door and turns on the light, wincing at the glare and the shabby sight of himself at dawn. He takes a piss, scratches his chest, yawns widely like a boy. He fills a glass with water and stands by the small window to drink it, staring through the frosted pane at the yellow-tinged wavering city. Already, through the glass, he can feel the temperature of the coming day. Already he hears car horns and the far-off grinding of a truck's gears. He has always liked the early morning: he thinks differently at dawn, there's a precision to his thoughts that isn't always there at the end of his long days. Standing by the hotel window, following the darting flight of the day's first birds, he knows that he should not come back to this room tonight: also that he will. He knows he should end

---

it, but also that he won't. He would like to return to the level and unmarked life he lived before: but she has left a rough-edged scar on him, black and awful as a cigarette burn.

It is he who says they can't go anywhere or do anything, but it's she who has lain awake thinking about it. He says it must bore her, this little cage they share; then phones her from the movies, the supermarket, a playground, another state. There is sometimes a burble of voices in the background, things he must turn from the telephone to attend. She looks down at the floor while she waits for his attention to return, scuffs the floorboards with her bare heel. Waiting, she thinks there must be few moments of silence in his life – his is a crowded existence, each minute of his time accountable. That isn't how life is for her. Almost always she is drifting, thoughtless, home when he rings, alone to speak safely on the phone. Their lives are intrinsically not the

———

same. At first she'd thought it endearing, his worrying that she would be bored, his imagining she needed the kind of amusement one could pay for, attend, critique. It seemed he was forgetting who she was, *what* she was. Participation is not really her style: more than that, she's ceaselessly aware who she is to him, the compartment she inhabits in his world. *The story will always be about him*. Freedom, normality – it would be illogical to expect these, it is against the nature of things. So at first she had smiled when he talked of restaurants and visits to galleries, midnight sessions at the cinema and weekends in the countryside, glimpsing in his words the wooing he had done in the past, his idea of how it should be done. And she'd been charmed and flattered that he would, if he could, apply such traditions to her.

Something has changed now, though. She has lain awake thinking too often, tunnelled deep beneath his words at daybreak, and now she thinks differently. Now she sees he isn't growing restless on her behalf, but rather on his own. The cage – the walls of her house, the walls of her cunt, the shaky old frame of her heart – is all she's allowed to give him; but, to him, it no longer seems like enough.

———

She sits on her bench in the park, a favoured perch from which her view sweeps a great distance of unmown grassland and she can see the approach of friends and enemies long before they're anywhere near; she has time to sit up and wave if she's feeling sociable, or whistle her dog and disappear. She thinks of it as her bench, feels generous when she shifts over to let an acquaintance share. Her dog stands on the bench beside her, careful not to affectionately touch her; he stands ears-up and statuesque, aware of his appearance, posing for Michelangelo. She has never heard it, but she guesses there are people in the park who tut when they see a dog with its feet on a seat.

Sometimes she has wondered what she would do if, sitting here on the bench one day, staring across the wide hills and green valleys of the park, she saw his spare familiar frame in the distance, recognised the stride that is never loping or lazy cutting a path through the seedy summer weeds. At first she wouldn't believe it, she would think she had mistaken someone else for him. But he wouldn't slow or deviate, he'd walk on with certainty toward her, and her dog's attention would be caught by the apparition, he'd freeze watchful, ears skyward, unblinking. As the

———

figure drew nearer she would sit up straighter, scowling, too incredulous to wave a hand. Her heart would be thumping and jumping skittishly. *Who is it?* she'd ask her dog, the same thing she asks when his car hums to a halt outside her house. Her dog would not doubt what he saw. He'd spring from the bench and fly across the paddock like a terrorist, ears flat and tail streaming, jaws unslung to the hot wind. Her dog doesn't love this man who visits, watches and waits for any chance to nip the hand that holds hers; nonetheless it is important to claim the visitor lest another dog do so, for in the park ownership is everything. The man in question is unperturbed: he laughs to see the hound coming like a werewolf closing in for the kill, smacks his thigh encouragingly, calls the animal's name. By now she would be crossing the grass, grinning stupidly, hardly believing her eyes; the dog would romp past him before circling broadly, warbling a song of hello. She'd put a hand to her mouth and ask, *What are you doing here?* He would shrug and smile boyishly, as if there were nothing to explain. *I felt like a change of scenery*.

Cross-legged on the bench, she smiles. She has seen it all happen in front of her eyes, her gaze still rests where he

———

stands. But her dog is sitting next to her and they're alone, there are midges and bushflies in the air that swells around them, it would not happen in real life.

This afternoon she had filled the bath to its brink and poured in too much bubblebath, a sickly green syrup that had smelled nauseatingly sweet. She'd run the water boiling hot, but it had cooled a degree by the time his car pulled up outside. 'Where are you?' he'd called, as he came through the door, but she had not answered, let him find her on his own. He'd stopped in the doorway of the bathroom and laughed at the bubbles, a great spiderwebbed mass of froth that had banked like snow and was oozing onto the floor. Crouched on the tiles she had looked up at him, chewing her lower lip. 'I think I put in too much.'

'It doesn't matter,' he told her. 'Ouch, hot,' he said, when he'd dropped his clothes to the floor and dipped one exploratory foot into the bubbles; but it couldn't have been too bad because he stepped in and sat down and the bubbles bloomed around him to his chin, he had almost disappeared. He scooped a single bubble to his mouth and pretended to eat it, and she smiled. 'Aren't you coming in?' he'd asked.

'I don't think there's room.'

'Hop in,' he replied, drawing up his knees.

So she had shaken off her dressing-gown and stepped intrepidly into the bath, gasping at the heat of the water, the bubbles making a crepe sound as she hunched down into them. The room was steamy, the walls weeping, she felt a tepidness in her lungs. He carved a path between the bubble-mountains with his hands, pressed his wet palms to her face. 'There is room,' he said. 'There's enough room.'

He had let his fingers slide down her chin and they vanished in the froth: they travelled over her breasts invisibly, touching their tips to her nipples. 'Come here,' he whispered, and drew her onto his lap, pushing up into her as the bubbles shrivelled and exploded. She put her arms around his shoulders and held close to him, a slick of bubblebath between his chest and hers, a smear of steam-sweat reflecting under their eyes. When she kissed him she tasted the bubble he'd eaten, the pop of it on his lips, and she had felt such a surge of love for him then, for his childish humour, his irresistible silliness. 'Tell me how it feels,' he'd said, and she answered, 'I love you.'

———

He had nodded, kissed her quickly, said, 'Tell me,' again.

She'd propped her chin on his collarbone. To have him inside her as fully as he could be – how did it feel? Like a kind of gorgeous punishment. Like being staked into the earth. Like, maybe, how death should feel, if there is any justice to life. A peeling, a pulling apart; a hard good invasion, a punch that made her want to punch back; a divine stabbing, perhaps, a wound she would die from, bleeding to death but not before she'd sunk her teeth into his arteries, skinned him alive. Whenever she did bite he would writhe and yelp, and in the fever of fucking him she could never understand why. There was black driving pleasure in mortal pain. There was soaring desire to injure and expire. His cock plunging high inside her, ramming and sliding and ramming stubbornly again: it felt like nothing and everything, like time dragged to a standstill.

She had rocked on his hips, felt the anchor of him in her, murmured her answer in his ear. He had lowered his eyes, blind to the buoyant landscape, and smiled as the words sank into his memory. She had kissed the leonine curve of his ear and crashed a hand down through the bubbles, snatching him up like treasure.

———

Now, in the park, she brings her wrist to her face and sniffs the leftover tinge of apple bubblebath. She feels washed pure, pared back, heated from the inside. She wonders how he is feeling, wherever he is now. These days he seems burdened by padlocks and chains and anguishes too heavy to haul through the long grass of an urban paddock. She worries, but pointlessly – it doesn't change anything. Her dog leans forward, watching something closely, nothing she can recognise.

He slams the door back so hard that it hits the wall, detonating a small explosion of plaster and paint. She steps backward, blinking fast; he grips her forearms and pushes her against the hallway wall even as the door is swinging on its hinges, shutting them from sight of the street. He holds her to the wall with his body, his fingers dug bruisingly in her arms, and kisses her harshly, his teeth knocking against hers, tearing at her lip. She snarls in protest, tries to turn her head away, and the bristles of his face rake her cheek and chin. He tightens his grip on her arms, feels the flesh and thin muscles give; with a hand on her jaw he pulls her face to his, forcing his tongue into her mouth. She chokes, kicks the wall with a heel, moves to

———

kick him: he steps adroitly out of harm's way without loosening his hold. 'Don't,' he warns, and she glares at him with rage in her eyes. Her cheeks are blotched, her lips shine. Her mouth is crooked with insolence. He thinks about slapping her face, but doesn't. Instead he jerks her away from the wall and shoves her the few strides into the bedroom. She stumbles a little, but he doesn't let her fall. She'll do only what he wants her to do. 'Lie down,' he says.

Defiance twists her mouth. 'No.'

His fingers clenching, he feels the bones in her forearms, sturdy, unbreakable. 'Don't make me kick you down.'

'You'll have to,' she breathes.

Instantly he swings an ankle, knocking her feet from under her. She goes down on her knees with a bark of dismay and he's there, a hand to her chest, forcing her to the floor. She sprawls on the carpet, fighting like a cat, her flying claws aimed for his eyes. He looms over her, pinning with difficulty first one, then the other, of her knees. Both of them are panting. She bares her teeth as if she'd shred him, and wrestles beneath his weight, eelishly agile,

———

unexpectedly brave. He's infinitely stronger than she is, they both know she cannot win, yet she fights like a cougar anyway, he dares not take his eyes from hers. When her nails gash him across the throat he is stung and, for a moment, truly frustrated and angry: he snares her wrists and grinds the scant bones together and sees, with satisfaction, the pain needle in her face. 'Don't do that again,' he hisses. 'I'll hurt you.'

'Screw you,' she replies.

He stares down into her varnished eyes – her hair is strewn over her face, her lips are parted and swollen. Her lashes are as dark as the wings of a crow, her eyes are imperfectly blue. Alone, at home, he has trouble remembering these details of her. He looks past her knotted hands to her chest, sees a shirt button undone, a triangle of pearly skin. He's catching his breath and she lets him, lying motionless between his thighs. The moment his sights return to her face she struggles, her legs wrenching out from under him, an elbow veering for his nose. He fights her down, swearing, feels with peculiar panic the shrill threat of her escape and, lower, an age-old growl that starts in his stomach and rumbles through his limbs

———

and speeds the flow of his blood, a feeling unknown yet recognised, a sensation he will never admit to, and not forget. Something within him wants to exhaust her, mar her, make tears come to her eyes. He wants to scar her and the primitive growl says he may: he was born to do this thing. The purpose of his living is to shove her to the floor and fuck her against her will.

And he's horrified by how easy it is, by the fact that he instinctively knows how to do what's required to bring her down, keep her down – as if he's practised at this terrible thing: he, a civilised man. Horrified, more than anything, by how agreeable it is, this thrumming, powering, lava-red growl – how steadfastly it sides with him, approves of him, presents itself as decent and trustworthy as a friend.

His cock is rigid, snagged painfully beneath his clothes; looming over her, he kisses her untidily, one hand still clamped round her wrists. She feels his cock butting against her hipbone. He pulls apart the zip of her trousers and drags the material down her legs, only far enough to expose her underwear. There are flowers printed on her pants, a pattern he's never seen. Their colours make him feel fractured, he cannot look at them. He works his hand through the spiny field of her hair and hooks two fingers into her cunt. She whines and struggles lamely, but he doesn't set her free; he pumps his fingers in and out of her, his knuckles striking bone, until the back of his hand is greased with her and her underwear has been bunched at her thighs. She doesn't fight him; her spine bends and her fingers claw, but she makes no sound. He is breathing raspily, faster than she; there's sweat dewing at his temples. Keeping her pinned with his elbows and knees, he undoes his belt quickly and yanks down his jeans. She starts to quietly plead with him, shaking her head, and tries to keep her legs together, her knees crushed against one another. He ignores whatever she is saying, leans his weight on her chest so she can hardly breathe; he forces a knee between her own and her legs narrowly splay. A shady gap opens and he shoves his prick into her, pushing in as high as he can. She gives a small, defeated cry; he bites his teeth into her shoulder and thrusts fast and hard. He's fucked her many times, but this is good and new. Everything is tight – the bondage of their clothing, the scratchy space through which he slides, the walls of her cunt which grab him like they'd kill him, the strained

———

muscles of her throat. Her thighs are greasy with his marauding, she's struggling feebly – he thinks of ropes and blindfolds, the things he could have done. He twists on her, spears in on an angle, slams through her viciously. His eyes are closed, his teeth in her throat; he tastes skin and collarbone, feels her wheezing in his ear. He jabs at her, counting: five, ten, fifteen. The growl is gone, he's thinking nothing, feeling only the strike of his cock against the dead-end interior of her, the lightning of his balls slapping flesh. Her wrists are still imprisoned by him, her arms pulled over her face. His hand goes under her shirt and yanks her bra from her breasts: he gouges into mounds of soft flesh, squeezes a nipple, pierces in his nails. Twenty, twenty-one, twenty-two. He kicks her with his booted feet, sucks ferociously at her neck. Something rushes through him like an adder: 'Scream,' he says, and she does: she tips back her head and howls. It's not a howl of grief or outrage, but a sound like life might make: vital, bloodthirsty. He clamps his arms around her chest and feels the vibration within her: in juddering bursts his come lunges from him as if rushing to meet the sound, to spin around it, cling to it, follow where it goes.

———

'Hold me,' he whispers: 'hold me,' and she does. She folds her arms across his waist and brings him close to her. Her throat and shoulder are throbbing from his bites, will be bluely bruised by nightfall.

It's long minutes before he collects himself, shifts his weight from her ribs to his elbows. Inexplicably, he can't look at her. 'I didn't hurt you, did I?'

'No.' She notes his shyness, smoothes his hair over his eyes. Her spine is scorched with carpet-burn, her wrists feel loose and snapped, but she isn't really hurt. In fact, she wants to giggle, to bounce around the room and jump on the bed, kiss him a hundred times. 'Thank you,' she says.

'Well,' he says, 'I guess it was my pleasure,' but he isn't laughing, nor even smiling. Indeed, he's filled with sadness, that other ancient friend. He sits back on his haunches, feeling about for his belt. He's desperate for a cup of tea, a resumption of the way things should be.

———

At the height of summer she sits down to write a story that will cool him as he slumps at his desk—

He didn't expect to see anyone on the beach, let alone her. It's a cold day, the first spine-chilling day of the year. She's wearing a hat and a thick winter coat and doesn't look like her usual self. Theirs has been a summery thing, though until this moment he hasn't realised how much so. Stuffy afternoons, the heat simmering up from footpaths, the doorknob warm under his touch: the sun has always shone on them. They've lain so often on the bed, on the floor, on the garden bench: rarely under blankets. He's not used to seeing her ponderously dressed, anchored by bulk

———

to the ground. From this distance she seems like someone different; but he is glad she won't be cold. He is glad it is her.

That is what he would say, were someone to interrogate him: he hadn't expected to see anyone on the beach on such a day. The wind is daggerish, and steely clouds are skulking in miserable gangs across the sky. Seagulls hover above the water, chequered wings hugging the gusts; a cargo ship on the horizon is stoically still. It's a day for depressives, weather for the alone. She strides through it confidently, covering ground while he dawdles. In her wake unspools a thread of prints, her boots pressing crimps in the sand. Her dog trots ahead of her, quick-stepping to be first to meet him, its muzzle glittered with seaspray.

When she's close, he smiles. 'Fancy seeing you.'

Her hands are in her pockets, bundled into chilly fists. She wears a black hat that's sprinkled with dots of silvery sand. She frowns at him quizzically from below its upturned brim. 'You invited me here.' She looks over the slate sea. 'It's freezing. It's like a bloody Bergman film.'

He feels he must protest, defend this landscape that he loves. 'It's wonderful though – the beach, in this weather.'

———

'Yes.' She shrugged, or that's what he assumed she did. There wasn't much to see of her beneath the coat and hat: he can't imagine her bare brown feet within such stout boots. 'It's shipwreck weather,' she says. 'It's good.' She has never quite made him understand that she herself is wintry – that windswept has always suited her, that she really only likes the coast when the ocean is tempestuous, the sand an empty pocked expanse of stony gold and grey. He thinks she is a creature of light and sunshine, but she is not. If she is anything she's earth, coal, rain. She remembers her uncle folding her hand in his own in the hours before he died. She had run through a frigid dusk to reach him and had carried with her into the hospital bedraggled roses and wisps of evening frost. 'Your hand is cold,' her uncle had said: 'Yes,' she'd answered. 'It's winter outside.' Those were their last words – she can't remember anything else that was said. She thinks her uncle was glad to feel the weather a final time, to have that wildness brought into the room.

'Shall we walk, or shall we sit down?'

She looks away from the water, to him – his face is tinted by the cold, smudged along the bones. She has

always loved the look of him – there is, for her, a restful-
ness in the very sight of him. Something that reminds her
of the agile skim of a lean canoe over shade-dappled
water. 'We'll walk.'

He smiles with quick approval – he feels a need to
keep moving. 'Remember,' he says, 'if anybody sees us, we
just happened to meet. A coincidence, that's all. I'm just
out taking an innocent stroll.'

'I remember,' she says.

'I'm sorry,' he says, the words pulled from him without prior consideration, and she smiles but doesn't reply.
And he is sorry: there's not an aspect to their acquaintance
that he doesn't somehow regret. Sometimes he wishes he
had never met her, that he could rewind time to the days
before she drove like a splinter under his skin and maybe
avoid her, scratch her out of existence. It's difficult for him
to remember the way he'd lived before she barnstormed
into his world. He thinks of her as dropping from the sky
like a devil or a spy, trailing a spiky tail or a parachute of
ballooning silk, descended from wherever, with him, like
a target, imprinted in her mind. He feels, sometimes, like
a hunted man, that time scrapes by like sandpaper, that his

days are hourglasses of dread. Yet none of this is anything he'd tell her, for fear she would go away. She has always, from the very start, maintained he only need say the word. Not a day goes by when he doesn't hold that word in his hand, taste it, feel its calamitous power. He struggles to recollect his old way of life. He's sure he would be happy if he had never met her, but he can't remember if, back then, he was what one might call happy.

She's been throwing a stick in the water for her dog, careless of the sand and seaspray. She is keeping the distance he insists upon, lest they should be seen. 'I am sorry,' he says again, because the stringy frustration that tangles his thoughts is tightening, his nerves are filed raw. 'This is all my fault.'

She picks up the stick and throws it – sand tears through the air, the dog racehorses away. He knows that the fault isn't all his own, but she won't tell him again. 'Yeah,' she says, her eyes on the dog.

'I don't want to lose you.' He can't return to a life he doesn't remember living. 'I don't know what's going to happen. Nothing good, I think.'

She glances at him, squinting against the milky sky's

———

glare. 'Since the day this started, you've never stopped talking about the day it will end.'

Transient: *it's what he once called himself, a word that had taken their breath away when he'd spoken it aloud. That undated last day has become his familiar, the raven that flies in his wake.* 'I will miss you. I'll never see you again, will I?'

'No,' she says: *he will not.* 'Because I will miss you too.'

'If things were different –' *He'd like to explain, but she looks back at the dog in the waves, saying,* 'They're not different – you won't make them be, so they can't be. Stop saying it.'

He's the worst mistake she has made in a long time. Everyone had warned her, and it wasn't that she didn't believe what they said. Everybody loses: you most of all. You'll live in the shadows, at the bottom of the list: you'll be the first sacrifice he makes. *She's not unwise, she had suspected these things. But she did not know, back at the start, the small things that would endear him – the lilting laugh, the kid-like pleasure in chocolate, his habit of inventing nicknames, the pride he takes in what she does. When she gives him up, she will feel his loss like a canyon carved out of her. She will miss the smell of him, the warm encompass of his hands. She will miss the eager beat of her heart in the hours before he arrives, the sheepishness that still lingers when they meet at the door anew. She'll miss his sharp-eyed attention to anything new in the house, to the rearrangement of the old things he likes. She will miss the slide of her shirt over her head, his hips moving between her thighs, the push of him inside. She'll miss his whispers, his arms cradling her; she'll miss lying beside him, watching him watch the ceiling, the sorrow in seeing the gravity of his situation settle into creases across his brow. He has been valiant and funny, harsh and moody, mischievous and playful. He has been like a paper crane to her, exquisite, complicated, folded, unfoldable. She would tell him that, even when she is gone, she will still be somewhere for him, that he could always find her again; that she will eternally, soundlessly, grievingly miss him. 'Tell me a joke,' she says, because he loves telling jokes, and she needs to look away from what she sees.*

He hurries to catch up to her, to walk by her side. He thinks for a serious moment, then asks, 'Why couldn't Johnny ride a bike?'

She has the stick, the dog is frisking at her feet. 'Why?'

'Because Johnny was a fish.'

She scoffs, chucks the stick, turns a scornful nose up at him. 'That's not a joke!'

He looks supremely untroubled. 'It's a joke for intellectuals. I wouldn't expect you to understand.'

'You're an idiot,' she tells him, and he answers, 'I know you are, but what am I.'

She laughs, shakes her head, the dog clambers from the water like a dragon, stick triumphant in jaws. A wave takes the opportunity to sidle up and slather her boots, making her jump sideways and yell. He's still smiling, delighted with his joke and suddenly delighted with this day; he spins on his heels and looks over the distance they've come, sees footprints etched cleanly in the sand.

—and at his desk he wipes his eyes, wondering where they go from there.

He lays a hand against her face. 'Open your eyes. Look at me.'

She opens her eyes and looks at him. Her eyes are not a pure blue. Tipped with fragments of hazel, green and grey, they're a shade that just fails to be fine. He never tells her she is pretty; he's unsure if he considers her to be so. He knows that he isn't here because of what she looks like – he is not a moth to a flame, hopelessly besotted by a sumptuous glow. Indeed, when he considers her closely, he sees she is a collection of faults: nevertheless it is she who haunts him, restively and mercilessly. It's she whom he carries everywhere. He wants to touch with his finger-tips the tiny images of himself that are wavering in the charcoal centres of her eyes. He wants to be that close to her – inside her, looking out. 'Talk to me,' he says. 'Tell me something.'

She looks up at him with languid gentleness, saying nothing. Her palms brush light as blossoms across his ribs. She cups his face in her hands and kisses him, her tongue skirting the edge of his teeth. There's always a dangerous bitingness in even her loveliest kisses: he is always afraid of being marked by her, a branding that won't wash away. She draws a breath and her chest rises: he feels the internal strength of her as if he rides a wave, strong lungs, strapping heart. 'Something about what?' she asks.

'Something about you and me.'

She blinks, then smiles indulgently, as if he's told an ordinary joke. He feels her naked feet shift against his knees, the closing of her thighs around his hips. Mostly he feels the calm embrace of her cunt, and the purr that travels through his cock, along his spine, that nuzzles behind his neck. Her hair is straggly across the pillow; he smooths strands away from her face. She cuts her hair herself, and this pleases him. He likes the way she is, self-sufficient. He likes it, how unnecessary he is to her. He likes to hear stories of the life she lived before he was here. If the stories are tragic or frightening he wants to stroke her head consolingly, as though she were a pup. But he also likes knowing that she survived such distresses without his help, that she's a rugged thing.

But now, his slender frame resting against her, his cock moving stealthily into her and gliding down until he is almost free, until the head of his cock touches her delicately and her back stiffens with the subtlety of it, he wants her to tell him something that does not leave him out. He wants to be in her eyes, her body, her mind. She tells him the same stories a hundred times, a boredom he endures with grace: but she also tells him things he has never heard before, never even imagined. She gives him words like gifts that he unwraps and is often startled, sometimes transported, sometimes distressed, by what he finds. She gives him gifts he can talk about to no one.

'Something about you and me,' she echoes: she's pretending to contemplate but he knows she has the story already, that she is nothing if not an actress. Her hips lift, tilting him steeply. He draws out of her, the peak of his cock noses her, he feels the stringy grapple of her hair. The air seems cool around him, although the room is warm. He pushes into her with force, his fingers rippling the sheets. She has closed her eyes again, hidden her face in his chest. Her hands glance off his slim flanks, her feet tuck under his shins. 'I don't want you to die,' she says. 'I don't want you to get old. I want you to stop: stay the way you are. Don't go far from me.'

He thinks about this, and smiles, and brushes her cheek tenderly. He puts his face next to hers to feel the flicker of her lashes. He runs a hand down her body and eases a finger into her cunt. Her skin there is carmine, he knows. A sheen of her serum coats her, and clings to the shaft of his cock. He touches his balls and it's an electricity that he doesn't dare repeat. He will bring her a photograph, perhaps, of himself as a boy, a lanky teenager, a thoughtful scholar. He is not a man who talks about his past; she places much faith in material goods, but she's never seen the possessions he has gathered over the years. The life he's led is beyond her reach unless he chooses to show and tell. He could be anyone, he realises: show anything, tell whatever. Create for himself and her a swashbuckler, a thief, a hero, a saint.

———

Her hand is slipping down his shoulder and spine, fluttering in the cleft of his arse. 'I don't believe in heaven,' she says. 'I can't think of anything worse. What a crowd. What a bore.' Her hand is a small bird, her fingers are wings, her nails are fragile sparrow claws when they skitter up his spine. 'If there were a heaven,' she says, 'it would be a different place for everyone. Every person would go to a heaven that was made just for them. They'd be the guest of honour for eternity.'

He is listening, aware of her breathing, the solidity of her breasts under his heart, the sound of her voice, the travels of her hand. When he slides into her he feels the amphibious sides of her, the sheer wall far within. His testicles touch her and she dunks a hand under her leg to keep them close to her. 'What I imagine is this,' she says. 'Walking down a path and there are gates, ancient iron gates, and there are trees and grass and birds, and an old stone wall that's mouldery, and there's ivy rambling around. There must be a river somewhere; it's a sunny day, fragrant, but this place is overgrown, a woodland, dim with shade. The path is stone, old as time. Beyond the gates people are waiting, watching me approach, and they're smiling; they've got drinks in their hands and some of them are lying on blankets in the grass and slouching against the trees and there's such a sense of kindness and peace, of happiness. I know who the people are: everyone I've loved, everyone I've lost. My grandmother: I haven't seen her since I was twelve. When my old dog died I asked her to hold him in her arms and care for him until I saw them both again. Walking down the path I see her, and she's smiling, and my dog wriggles out of her arms and comes sprinting to me, fast and young and strong. Not only him – all my animals. My cats, my dogs, my birds. They fly past the gates and swirl around me; I get down on my knees and I'm crying: I have longed to see them again. They come with me along the path, frolicking, arguing, playing. When I reach the wall I see the gates are tall and rusty, the paint is peeling off them. They're listing on their hinges and the gap between them is small. The ground underfoot is stony and mossy, maybe slippery – I need to be careful. I don't want to fall. So I step forward, watching my feet, and as I duck between the gates a hand reaches out to me, someone wanting me to be safe. I take the hand and it holds me up, I don't slip on the stones, I'm

———

safe; and only when I'm standing there, on the other side of the gates, and people are strolling over to meet me, do I look around to see who it was, the one who helped me through. And it's you: you're wearing this sloppy old comfortable suit and your hair is hanging in your eyes. You wink at me, and smile, and nod to say you'll be sitting under a tree somewhere, having drinks with friends you've made. And I just feel such an – amazing – *joy* – seeing my animals, these long-lost people, this wonderful place, you. I think *Finally: finally everything is all right now*.'

Her eyes look away from the window, and rest on him. 'Your heaven won't be like that,' she says.

'No,' he agrees; he feels emptily sad. 'You will be there, though.'

She smiles, shifts her cooling body, tightens her muscles so a shock flares through him, stiffening his cock within her. 'I love you,' she says.

'I know it,' he replies. 'You're beautiful.'

She laughs, as if that's funny; then rolls him over abruptly, carrying him inside her, and the linen is sleek against his shoulders, the blankets velvety against his face. She pulls the doona over them and it comes down like a

———

cloud, bringing cloisteredness and a fuggy puff of air. She'd be the devil in the corner of his private heaven, the one to whom his eyes would nervously flit. She sits astride his hips and fucks him until it exhausts them, until, like a cat in darkness, she screams.

———

The drug they have taken is like a truth serum. She sits cross-legged on the bed, playing cards; he sits behind her, the pillows bolstering him, holding her between his knees. He is brushing her hair with a small plastic brush; he parts the locks with his fingers and puts his lips to the down on her neck. She still bears a remnant of the summer that's ended, a half-moon of tan where the sun snuck past the collar of her t-shirt. When he touches the freckled skin there he thinks he feels something that has never been felt before. His heart is hammering, though on the outside he is calm; inside he feels alertly excited, and remotely afraid.

The cards are spilling messily on the rumpled quilt.

———

She turns one of them over, scans the ramshackle row. 'Tickle my back,' she says.

His fingers are stroking the crest of her neck. He answers with closed eyes: 'No.'

'Please,' she says. 'No one tickles my back.'

He drops the hairbrush over the side of the bed, hears it bounce cheaply away. He slips his arms around her, trapping her arms to her sides. The cards in her hand bunch in awkward angles, but she doesn't protest. Her sight glides over the rows she's laid down; she feels she has made a mistake. 'I'm all alone,' she adds absently. 'There's no one to tickle my back.'

She is wearing navy, just a fine cotton shirt, though the room, like the day, is cool. He is wearing her dressing-gown, a bulky vividly-coloured thing that pulls up short above his wrists but rucks in a kingly fashion around him. He runs a palm down her back, rides airily over the slant of her ribs. He feels her spine, which reminds him of a fish. There are soft pads of fat on her hips, although lately she has been growing thin. The venetian blinds clatter on a chill draught; amber leaves are shed from the trees. He had brought her, as an offering, the heart-shaped skeleton of a birch tree's leaf, its bare frame as intricate as a city seen from the sky. He had known she would like it, and was happy when she did. His touch is raising goosebumps all the way up her flanks. He says, without forethought, 'You take advantage of me.'

She sweeps up the cards she had set on the bed, shunts the pack tidily together. 'How do you mean?'

'My kindliness,' he says. 'You take advantage of my kind nature.'

She smiles to herself, languidly. 'Why not.'

'You take advantage of the fact that I'm a man, and weak because of it.'

It's a surprising thing to say – he had not known he was going to say it. He waits curiously to hear how she'll reply. It is a minute before she says anything; he wants to query, *Has the cat got your tongue?* 'Do you say such things to hurt me?' she asks.

His fingers cruise the knobbly fishing-line of her spine. 'You want to hurt *me*, don't you? Hasn't that been your plan all along?'

She shrugs as if she couldn't care less. 'How do I intend to hurt you?'

'You'd take everything from me. You'd leave me with nothing, bereft. You are like a dog-bite, a vampire: you're a bloodsucking bat.'

She is not the type to be easily insulted: she supposes what he says is his truth. The view through his eyes must be very different from the world she sees through her own. 'I have always told you – from the very start – that when you want freedom, I'll set you free.'

'How decent of you, how bloody gracious. When I am free, you will be gone.'

His caress makes her shiveringly tense. 'Isn't that what you want? For me to be gone? It's what I know you wish, sometimes.'

'No. You're stupid, you don't understand. I want you to stay, and I want you to go.'

'. . . You're as contrary as a girl.'

'No. I am weak as a man.'

She licks her dry lips; she has not laid out the cards. His fingers run easily around her ribs and scoop the crescents of her breasts. Her nipples are hard, he has made them so. She feels his cock against her, firm at the cleft of her arse. Her throat is arid with the drug's bitterness. Her

———

nose runs and she sniffs uncouthly hard. 'Tell me what else,' she says.

'Sometimes I hate you.' He pets her with elegance, as he does most things. 'Sometimes I think I want to kill you. You bore me; you're tedious; you're repetitive. You never listen to what you say; I don't listen to most of it anyway. This house is like my prison cell. You're a disease I have caught and can't shake.'

'I would set you free,' she reminds him. 'I'm not your keeper. You have only to ask.'

'There, you see! I am nothing to you. You made me want you – you ruined me. But you must not love me much at all, if you'd set me free on a word.'

The cards are angular and unsympathetic in her hand. 'I must love you more than I love myself,' she answers. 'When you are gone, I will be alone.'

The drug is surging through him, plucking his thoughts from brilliant thin air. He feels lordishly thespian, he is on a stage. 'You say you are used to being alone, so what difference would my leaving make to you? *None*. Your life would resume just the same as before. And if my absence would make no difference, it means I

———

am nothing to you. You don't love me, though you say you do.'

'You don't love me,' she says quietly.

He pauses, rests his chin on her shoulder, thinks about this. 'Once,' he muses, 'I thought I did. It was fleeting, I'm glad to say. I'm glad I didn't do anything rash for you. I thought I was going to, I nearly did: I'm pleased I saved myself. I'm pleased I did not give up everything that is precious in exchange for you, a lowly bloodsucker.'

'. . . I have never asked you to give up anything. I have never asked anything from you.'

'But you do!' He shakes her. 'Don't you see? You do! You ask for a great slice of me – you demand it! And if I don't give it, you sulk and cry, your feelings are drearily hurt. I have to sit at my desk and feel ashamed and try to discover where I went wrong. And worry that this time you'll leave me, that I'll never hold you again. But I am just another of your stupid toys, these expensive things you buy on a whim and never touch lovingly again. I am behind glass, like them; you look at me as you look at them, coldly, indifferently.'

She licks her cracked lips, sucks down the sourness.

———

Sometimes she wonders if her heart has pieces left to break, blood enough to bleed another drop. 'I have had to keep you behind glass,' she says, 'because my touch is damaging to you. I would take you to bed with me every night, curl up with you in my blankets and sleep beside you, but I cannot. You don't belong to me. So I'd be foolish to let myself become too attached. Any day I might lose you, any hour. Can you imagine how that feels? Can you imagine how it is, to be forever on that verge – always wondering *when* you'll say the word, *when* you'll decide to be free? Fearing that every stupid thing I say might cost me that price? You say I'd remember how to be alone – you're right, I would. It's a skill I'd be a fool to forget. But don't talk to me about being alone: what would you know about it? Nothing. You don't know what lonesomeness is.'

'Don't speak for me,' he retorts. His cock is demanding things now, is a jabbering voice in his head. 'You know nothing about me.'

'I know some things.' Her eyes too are closed. 'I know that when I need you, you won't be here. Not when I'm hurt or tired or overjoyed, not when I ache for you, when tears fall down my face for you, your hush voice, your

———

kind heart, your pretty laugh: you won't be here. You don't belong to me – I know. You belong to others, and you're happiest that way.'

'You knew all this from the day we met.'

'Yes, that's true.'

'But you'd make me feel guilty for it anyway.'

'Yes, that's true too. It's inadvertent: I don't mean it. I'm glad you are happy somewhere, with someone, I don't want to take that from you . . . None of this has turned out how I thought it would. I have botched the job. I'm not very good at it, I suppose.'

He kneads her skin tranquilly – he isn't angry with her. He feels only a loose-limbed sense of regret and he's not certain what it is he's regretting, how deeply buried its roots are in the past. His jaw aches from the drug, his eyes are wide, his fingers and arms feel like splendid wings, the regal wings of a swan. If he looked to the ceiling he's convinced he would see maelstroms and fascinating designs. It is a lifetime since he's taken such drugs. It's good; he feels boldly young. He prods her with an elbow, says impishly, 'There are some things you do well. Not many, but some.'

———

'Take advantage of you? Do I do that well?'

He's reproducing the designs of the ceiling onto her back. He wishes, now, that he hadn't said those words. His hands glide over the bones of her hips and mould themselves around her arse. 'I am a dumb grass-eating beast,' he says, 'dragged down by a cleverer, fanged one. You can eat me: I won't fight. It's simply the way we are: it's how we were born to be.'

She's hanging her head, half entranced, smiling limpidly. His fingers sneak into her, dart puckishly away. 'I'm sorry I make you unhappy,' she says. 'I thought, when this started, that we'd laugh more than we do; and that everything would be easier. Not so many knives.'

'It's no laughing matter, being eaten alive. Seeing your guts spill out in a gory trail behind you.'

'Do you want to be free?' She leans against him, into his chest. He enfolds himself around her, his cheek rubbing her throat. 'You need only say the word.'

'Will you cry?' he murmurs. 'Will you hate me?'

'Yes, I'll cry: how could I resist one last tear at your vulnerable parts? I would cry until I couldn't stand, until there was nothing left of me. But I would never hate you.

———

I have loved you too much: and love doesn't die, not really. Not completely. Part of me will always reach for you.'

'Shut up, then,' he sighs. 'You bore me. Put the cards down, forget your game. I long to be inside you.'

He need only lift her shirt-tail to slide lovingly into her.

He is going away. She stands above him, stripped of clothes, the warmth of the gas heater baking her calves. She looks down, past her breasts and stomach, and thinks of him sitting on the aeroplane, his long legs poised awkwardly, frowning as he struggles to rest. He's been full of chatter about this journey, and she's listened and tried to be enthused. His hips are pinioned between her ankles, yet already he feels far away. He has told her he doesn't mind the travelling, that he'll blithely sleep for hours, yet she persists in imagining him wakeful, tormented, fatigued. She wonders how much of him is someone she has invented, pleasing herself.

For the moment he's laughing. 'What?' she asks.

———

'Look at you,' he says. He giggles like an exuberant child – he's sprawled, like an infant, amid the pleats of a lavish fur blanket. He blinks up at her, his hands starfished on her shins. Her legs are like a brown country road, the heat on them like sun on a dirt track; her knees are smooth country stones. His gaze is a beetle, flying up, scribbling down. The lips of her cunt sit primly across the flesh underneath – he thinks of a purse made of puckered satin, embroidery and pewter locks; of agate and diamonds and chips of mother-of-pearl. 'Standing like that,' he chuckles. 'I've never seen you upside down.'

She grins, poses jauntily, her hands on her hips. Her nipples are twin red nodules, upstanding and forthright – he has never seen them tender or retiring. He loves it, the way her body flares for him, he's reminded of cobras and peacocks. Her body shows off to him, plays all its enticing cards. He has never run a finger into her and not found her waiting, wet, for him. It's snatched the breath from him sometimes, to feel himself so wanted. Everything about her looks different from where he lies – her breasts rearing imperiously, her pubic hair a black battleground. Her face is veiled by falls of hair, like a martyr's face in a painting. If he could introduce her to his friends they would not see much in her, she's an ordinary scrap of a thing anyone would pass without pausing on the street: yet, to him, she's jewellish. Her eyes are sapphires, her touch is gold, inside her there is treasure. He scouts a hand up her leg, laces his way through the hair, explores the cavities of her. He's reminded of crustaceans, their pinkness and interlocking shells. She holds to the mantelpiece, smiling distractedly, flinching at something that isn't pain. He watches her face, liking to see what she feels. Funny, how nice it is to give pleasure. In his life outside these walls he seems to lurch from error to error, to satisfy no one, to cast a shadow of gloom. Here, though, he is angelic. Here is a space he manages to fit.

She gives a sharp squeak and jumps sideways – his hand is left hanging, fingers glinting in the heater's radiance. 'Did I hurt you?' he asks, knowing he hasn't, being polite. She ignores the question, steps over his leg, hunkers on the blanket between his knees. When she runs her hands along his calves it is with encouraging pressure, so his knees splay apart. He tucks his hands behind his head and peers down the length of himself, past the rise of his chest and the dip of his stomach, past his cock which points at him plaintively, bearing some unreasonable grudge. She makes him wait a high-strung moment before touching her tongue to his arsehole, and at the touch his spine arches, he clenches shut his eyes. He loves this, loves it, loves it. He'd been shocked the first time she had done it – startled and mortified. There'd been a dreadful instant of being close to tears, of reliving what it was to be a boy humiliated. He'd had to force himself to lie still, convinced he could never look her in the face again. But then something had travelled through him, a powdery snowfall – she was licking him softly, softly. Then, as now, his back had bowed. Then, and now, he wondered how he had endured living without the sensation. It was druggish: her tongue gliding over the knurled terrain of his anus is a feeling he would kill for. He is not one for moaning, but sounds sigh uncatchably out of him. She laps at him steadily, a cat at milk, her hands maintaining pressure on his thighs, absorbing the quiver of his nerves. He thinks of cottonballs, their absolute softness. Then her tongue becomes a pointy little arrow that prods him, pokes past the clinched rim of him, cavorts across his hot skin. He works his fingers into the blanket, swears mutedly. He doesn't want to disturb her. Her tongue goes over the brink of him, inside him, out again. It works at him, sucks him, pulls him reachingly toward her. *Sweet*, she'd told him, when he once gathered the courage to ask. *Sweet, I don't know why.*

She sits back suddenly, shaking her hair from her face; she closes a hand over his cock and tugs it, slips the other hand between her own thighs. He watches her slot three fingers into herself and swill them around. He feels shudders of excitement, his feet jerk expectantly. His cock seems zealous, straining to stand taller, as anxious and ambitious as a teacher's pet. When she lowers her head to take him into her mouth his view of her slicked fingers is blocked, but he knows what she means to do. He shuts his eyes and lies helpless, giving himself over to her. He feels the huff of the heater in the hollow of his armpit. She lulls him with tenderness – her lips encircle his cock's head and she suckles on him peaceably, her tongue moving soothingly over diaphanous skin. When she takes him fully into her he feels the lover's-leap at the back of her throat. It's good, it's dreamish, but he is waiting.

One buttery finger, her longest, pushes against the

muscle ringing his anus and forces its way past this defence with ease. She spears high into him, hears his cutting intake of air, feels his instinct to say or do something – protest, slam his legs together, spread them wider still. She strokes the satiny interior of him, kneading her finger into his walls as she sucks him, her tongue toying idly with the eye of his penis. She draws her finger almost out, feels the grasp of the muscle there and teases it, her finger dipping back and forth. She wants to suck him until he comes, but wants him inside her too, to feel the instant when his cock goes hardest and his orgasm blows through her like leaves. They see each other as often as always, which is not all that often, not as often as she'd like, but these days she is acutely aware of the fraying of his edges. He is a good man trying to do something bad, and it's wearing away at him: he is not careless enough to leave his morality waiting like a dog in the yard. One day these visits to her will cease – she senses that her fate is being decided in conversations she cannot join, in arguments where she can't speak in her defence. When he goes, it will probably be with scant warning. And she'll wish, that day and for a long time afterward, that she could feel him reach within her one last time.

So she slips her finger from him, crawls up and lies alongside him, lays a hand against his face. He smells himself on her fingers, a loamy odour, the underground, a stink that disgusts him. He rolls over without speaking, weighing her to the floor, takes himself in hand and penetrates her forcibly, as if nothing but vigour and haste will cure his prick's vile temper. She parts her legs gladly, welcoming him in; she laughs a little, not at him but at her need for him – at herself. He is absurdly precious to her – she shouldn't have let him become so. She wonders how she will survive his leaving, the agonising loss – if she's not, in fact, already the walking dead, dangling by the neck from a razor-tight string.

When he's on the windswept verge of coming he hunches against her, snarls loving words in her ear. She holds him tightly, lets him know he isn't alone. She feels the surge of strength in him, the pump and splutter of his warmth. She hugs him, rocks him, she loves him; she's stupid.

When he's recovered she brings an immaculate mandarin on a plate and he peels it deftly, puts piece after piece in her mouth. The room fills with the crystalline scent of citrus – he thinks this is how the dawn of time must have smelled. She agrees, it's a fantastic smell: but later she will put her palm to her face and seek from her fingers the preferable earthiness of him. She will search for him forever, when he's gone. She thinks of him on the aeroplane, sleeping soundly, winging his way back through time.

She looks out through fogginess, touches her fingers to glass iced with fog. She could write a message in the whiteness but she doesn't, for she knows words don't easily wipe away, that they stay preserved even when the cloak of steam has eroded into the pallid day and the shower-screen seems clear again – the words would be there, ghost letters on the glass, visible in a certain light and from a certain angle. She will not risk anyone seeing what she might, in a few seconds of weakness, inscribe in sweeping script on the glass. If he were here, showering with her, she might risk it just to please him, to see the amusement in his eyes as he followed the path of her thoughts. She contents herself with pawing at the screen like a fly at a door,

———

her fingertips leaving tracks that break off and mean nothing. It's satisfying nevertheless, to leave a mark, to have an effect.

When he is gone, the days seep painstakingly into each other; it's a matter of waiting. Everything is secondary to his absence. She laughs, talks, thinks, decides. She can hold a conversation, flip through a newspaper, cook herself a meal; she tries on clothes, walks the dog, watches the midday movie. But everything she does is done underwater – underneath the skimming fact that he is elsewhere, far. It is the fact that colours her world, or leeches the colour from it; the fact that skittles everything. This is what grieving is like, she knows. A life lived submerged, a constant struggle for oxygen. The incessant turning-over of an empty mind.

She looks down at herself, to the water pooled at her feet. She has never been proud of her body, though it is a decent and reliable thing. Almost always she thinks of it as an affable partner-in-crime. It has a hundred failings, yet she's aware that it does its best. She cares for herself less than she cares for her animals – she eats nothing she should, she never rubs in sunscreen, she gives no thought to her appearance unless there's someone to impress – but her body soldiers on regardless, forgiving, tough as nails. Her legs are strong, her feet aligned deadly-straight; blue veins course the pale undersides of her arms. Her hands are speckled from years of digging in sunshine, her nails kept practically short. Her breasts are far from spectacu-lar – they always look, to her, wayward, confused as to their purpose. She's not skinny, but there isn't much fat on her; perhaps a little too much on her belly. Her rump is overlookable, hardly jaunty. Her hair is fly-away, with a mindlessness of its own; she keeps her pubic hair trimmed strictly, for otherwise it's a jungle. It is not a pretty body, she's always known that: too short, too nondescript. It's a working frame, a pit-pony, honest, unadorned, buttressed by muscle, made for climbing, hauling, performing tasks. He is built like an egret, and maybe in his aesthete's mind he would prefer similar refinement in her. Yet she only need be near him and his cock rears up like an evangelist, wilful as a bloodhound, pushy as a salesman; she need only say a word to make him quaver, cast just one sugary glance to have him bite his lip. She wonders: how can two people so hopelessly drawn ever become free? She doesn't know who she is anymore. Her existence has been derailed. Her life is him, nothing else – nothing is as important as him, nothing's worth thinking of or waiting for. She feels like she's tumbling over and over through depthless ivory snow: her fall is cushioned, even picturesque, but nothing can save her from the broken freeze that's to come. Every day he struggles to wrench her claws out of him, wounding himself and her in the process – then lays himself down again willingly, unpredictably, just when she's about to drag her dislocated carcass to whatever dark hole can offer a desolate clawed creature some peace. And she's always overjoyed to have him back, they tell one another that life is pitch without the other, and their bloody struggle begins again.

She bends her head, lets the water hammer her shoulders. She always runs the shower too hot, so there's a stain of crimson under her skin. Ribbons of hair are slicked to her forehead and her cheeks. She runs a block of soap along her arms, across her stomach, over the rise of her breasts. A wash of water and soap-slime makes her skin gleam. The steam has made her nipples spongy and glowingly pink. She glazes soap onto her fingers and puts her fingers into her vagina, separating the pieces, opening herself out to the ministrations of the water. She remembers the day she discovered what her cunt was good for: she was a little girl, flat-chested and tomboyish, in a sweltering indoor swimming pool, taking lessons with her class. The water was deep, exhausting to survive: at the first opportunity she swam to the side of the pool and propped her elbows on the rim to rest. A dense jet of filtered water was powering out from a vent in the pool wall, and she let it pound into her stomach as an endless, turbo punch. She rose slightly on her arms, to sit her chin on the cool tiles, and the jet caught her between the legs. Immediately her body twanged with a pleasure that seared to her head and toes, stiffening her limbs, halting her breath, circling her eyes; she'd felt spellbound and stupefied, afraid she might wet herself or cry. The noise of her classmates, the splashing and shouting, the stench of the chlorine and the clamminess of the room all dropped away, there was only her and the *feeling*, the soupy muscular throb. The jet was strong enough to support her, to straddle like an iron bar, to push aside the crotch of her bathers with invisible churning knuckles; and she had rocked on it, letting it pummel her, begging it not to stop. Her breathing was surface, her eyes blind, her body was inflexible with bliss. She didn't hear the swimming coach blow the whistle, nor see the woman until she loomed above her with snapping fingers and clapping hands. She had swum away in a hurry then, joining the other children along the deep-end wall. Her face was blazing, she wanted to howl; probably nobody had noticed, probably no one guessed what she'd been doing, but she was sickly ashamed. She knew, without knowing how she'd found the knowledge, that the feeling was private, vulnerable, unbecoming. Yet all she had wanted to do was paddle back to the sorcerous jet, and hang before it forever.

Now, her fingers stroking her vulva, water streaming over her shoulders and down the inside of her legs, she chuckles at the memory: *dirty girl.* She should go back to that swimming pool, it's still there; maybe the jet of water is still ramming out of the wall, waiting like a faithful friend for her return. She pushes back the lips of her cunt, exposing her fleshy frills and the fish-eye of her clit. The water finds its way, thin streams coursing between her crannies, but it's sad, it's nothing. She needs him. She needs his face, his fingers, his lungs, his tongue, his gifted rummaging. Often when she kisses him she tastes herself on his lips, a bitter chemical taste these days, her natural smokiness subdued. She thinks it disagreeable, but he never complains. He burrows down the bed to find her, forcing her knees up, spreading her arse. Her spine bends for him: she misses him. She wonders if, for him, it has all just been about the screwing. He says it isn't – he swears he loves her. But she wonders if, when their fall through the gorgeous snow comes to its end, as everyone says it will, as everyone says it must, it will be her inane chatter, her domestic ineptitude, her face, her scent, her childish try-hard joking and good cheer, or the fucking he misses the most.

Why, she thinks: *why, why*.

He has been gone a long time – a week, which is the longest time. Her eyes ache with a need to see him again, he is the only source of beauty in the world. She remembers the time when they filled each other with delirious glee, when they carried one another as glittering secrets in their minds, when they were like sandstorms to each other through hot dishevelled afternoons. She could have given him up on any of those days and laughed lovingly at the memory of him forever, regretting nothing, enduring no serious loss: he'd have been like a fabulous comet in her skies. Now, if she must give him up, she will bleed. Her world will crash down to its knees. She will pack up and hide the small things he's given her, because she won't be able to bear the sight of them; and even when she's an old old lady she will keep them locked away.

Please, she thinks: *please, please.*

Don't.

A line of autumn's last sunshine is cutting a creamy dash through the window and the steam, spotlighting a square of the bathroom floor. Where he is, it is nighttime, but when he wakes it will be to a world lit by the same sun that's in the sky above her. She will dry herself in the shaft of light and maybe the sun will take away some memory of her in this single flourishing beam and find him wherever he is and wrap around him and warm him, cast his shadow. She wipes the marks of her fingers from the shower screen and turns off the taps.

He stands above the river, looking down. The morning sun has pushed the shadows out of sight, tucking them behind the stately legs of the bridge so the water spreads below him unblemished, torpid, grey. His hands hang loosely over the brink of the bridge wall, the bones of his wrists like round seashells at the cuffs of his coat. She once used a word to describe his wrists – he can't remember what it was. She has lavished him with admiration, draped him in gossamer cloaks of adoration, made him finer, beautiful. When he thinks of himself now, he is not thinking of the person he used to be. He is a changed animal, something from which the dust has been wiped, the gnarly edges chiselled back and made smooth. He gleams from

———

the inside now. But there's a seam of oil, too, a greasy leak in his heart that used not to be there. He glimmers, but for this corrosive flaw.

He stares down at the water, the morning breeze scudding the back of his neck. Every time he sees it he's startled over again by the width of this river, the grand excess of it. A magnificent waterway for such a pinched piece of land, great enough to carry away all the centuries of war and art and courage. From where he stands, the buildings on the twin riverbanks are distant enough to be dollhouses. Cars flash past behind him, and occasionally a striding pedestrian, but the bridge, like its river, is generous, made for isolation. Nothing need come close enough to touch him, he is disturbed by no thing. There are birds swooping the riverbank where the water congeals between cobbled walls and flat-bottomed boats, foamy and littered – white birds, maybe seagulls – if she were here, she could tell him what they were. She knows creatures, trees, their lyrical names; she knows how to create and repair things. Oddly antiquated knowledge, he's always thought – in this world, it's no longer necessary to know the titles of things or how they are made.

———

There must be cleverer matters in her mind, matters less worldly, more valuable: but they've rarely spoken of anything except their plight, the strange gloaming acquaintance they share. Everything about them has been surface: she even loves him with a dumb-dog devotion, with a lack of intelligence and refinement. She has drenched him in so much affection that he can afford to shake off some of it, leave it like tacky footprints in his wake. He'll never remember the whimsical word she used to describe his wrists.

This is an old country, and his memories of it are old. He was a child here, a teenager, a young man. He crossed this bridge as a boy, his fist balled in his mother's hand, shopping-bags swishing at her knees. She had cautioned him to stay close to this wall he now leans against, these stones that rasp his hip. Grown up a little, wandering the city alone, he'd run his fingers along the stones and felt their roughness nip away pieces of him. He remembers pondering how many thousands of discontented adolescents had done the same before him and what had become of them, poets, painters, admirals of ships. He wonders what he would say if, looking up, he saw the boy and the youth and the woman standing nearby, the boy's lips kissing the parapet, the teenager fidgety and irritable. He'd be embarrassed by the consideration of his younger selves; he'd feel a need to explain himself to his mother. *I am just a man now.* His mother would never have asked that he be more, yet he knows he has disappointed her. *You are just a man:* it's what's been murmured against his shoulder at times when he's been stricken, staring at the corners of her bedroom, sitting beside her on the garden bench. *You are not a bad man, you are only a man.* The words have been intended to console, anchor him – they never have. He looks away from ghosts, to birds. The important thing is to be a good man.

He bends slightly forward, his elbows on the weather-worn stone, his toes against the wall. The closeness puts agreeable pressure on his thighs and groin. Upriver he can see other bridges – he recites their venerable names in his mind. He knows she has been a tourist in this city – she speaks about it in an off-hand way that quietly offends him. This is a metropolis that is owed awe – it's a sign of her ignorance, he thinks, that she should dismiss the city as grimy, overrated, blighted by its population. If she ever crossed this bridge she would have stopped to watch the nosediving birds but she would have walked past the blue plaque that says someone famous once leapt from this very parapet he leans against, that a battleship limped home from war to sink in the familiar water beneath his feet. Like a cat, she would only have had eyes for the birds.

The breeze has picked up, and a film of fluid has smudged the focus of his view. There is something morosely satisfying in thinking harshly of her. It's easier to build a barricade against her when the gloss is scraped from her shine. Diminished and soiled, it's easier to turn her away, keep her out. He tilts his weight against the wall, puts his hands in his pockets and hugs his coat to himself. He's a dark, lone, windswept figure, the kind that has haunted this nation for centuries. He's Shelley, he's Heathcliff, he's every burdened man who has ever knocked the cap off a bottle of laudanum or swallowed a phial of cyanide. He remembers her saying she liked Byron when she was young, then grew up and discovered the poet to be a self-indulgent prat. She is an utter

———

barbarian. He's hard just at the thought of her, his cock pushing bluntly at his jeans. He brushes his knuckles, still gloved in the pocket, across the tip of his penis, and the jolt in his spine almost buckles his knees. She's here, rising over him, even when he is trying to burn her like a witch. She's a triffid that blinds him, a virus eating him alive. He shifts so close to the wall that its stones scuff his hip and knees; his hand, hidden by obliging folds of material, is jammed flat between the wall and his cock which is as achingly taut as it's ever been, heated beneath his cool palm. He stares upriver, his vision taking in the view, the ever-shortening assembly of bridges, the thread of cars crossing them, the birds and boats on the periphery, the lurch and drag of the water. He hears traffic behind him, the rushing footfalls, the ting of bicycle bells and laughter into mobile phones, the bullocky sigh of a bus. His thoughts are all inside himself, in the soothing liveness of his hand against his imprisoned cock, in his fingertips cupped around his balls, in the wall that is just like her, strong, something to push himself into, something against which to hide. She can lift her knees high, raise her cunt in the air, gape at him invitingly, tangled as the roots of a tree. He closes his eyes and tears slide between his lashes; his hand, his coat and his cock are burning, his blood is rushing and thin. He sees her flanks backing onto him, his cock disappearing as she comes; her arms, braced against the wooden bedhead, are as unyielding as oak, he thinks of fucking a forest, the rattling twigs, the creaking timber, the birds bursting into the sky. Half a world away from wherever she is, he fucks her in his mind. He wants to bend her over this wall and slam himself into her until the sun crosses overhead and casts their shapes onto the river, her oak-branch arms spread broadly, his lips kissing her wild hair. It will be easy to come, he knows. In less than a moment, he will come. He'll fuck her and then he'll let her plummet over the brink, down and down into the listless grey water, and she won't rise to the surface, he won't see her white face, her confusion, he won't have to witness any of that because she will not rise, the water will sweep her from his sight, the current will carry her away. When she is so completely doomed, he will be infinitely less so.

He comes with a lurch, a gulp of air between the teeth; his hipbone knocks jarringly against the wall. He blinks his eyes open, dares not look around, blood already colouring his cheeks. His spine is bent, his shoulders bunched; he straightens cautiously, his crooked arms falling to his sides. He's nervous for a minute, scandalised by himself, scrambling to think of an excuse. But then he sees that the world is continuing – that no one is stopping to accuse him. No one has seen him shunt her over the edge. *I had no choice*, he tells her, though the river will already have washed her away and she couldn't possibly hear. *I had to do it, you know I did*. Drown like a kitten, he begs of her: don't live like a cursed dog that forgives and forgets every terrible thing.

He clears his throat, wipes his mouth, shakes crumbs of mortar from his boots. His come is already unpleasant, cooling and gluey on his skin. He remembers she'd once folded his hand around himself and said, *Tell me how you do this alone*. He'd shown her carefully, taking his time. *I'm always thinking of you*. He brings his coat close, pushes away from the wall. The hem of the coat flicks his calves as he walks; he turns up the collar to keep the wind from his throat. She had given him a cake of swarthy soap as a going-away present: he'll go back to his room and shower. He had asked what she would like brought home as a gift, and she had asked, like a child, for chocolate. He will remember to buy it.

She is kneeling on the floor, her clothes shabby and eccentrically dappled with colour, the backs of her hands spotted blue. There's a spangling exultation inside her that is keeping her on her knees. 'I didn't think you'd come back.'

He shrugs. 'I nearly didn't. I thought about it. I shouldn't have.'

She nods, slinking past the sting of the words with her eyes averted and head down. She has never understood if he says such things with an intent to injure – if a satisfaction jet as a panther is licking its teeth even as he stands there – or if his world is simply a place of callous edges and he has never learnt that other worlds aren't the same.

———

She pictures him walking on a tundra of black onyx, climbing screedy hills of splintered quartz. 'What made you decide?'

He says, 'I haven't decided.'

Her smile falters; she glances at the paintbrush, thinks she must put it in water. She looks up at him briefly. 'And yet you're here,' she says, and laughs fitfully. 'Here you are.'

'Maybe,' he says wearily; it is difficult to look at her, this girl who is never quite the same in truth as in his daydreams. Again and again, she's a frustration to him. 'I shouldn't be. I wish I wasn't, actually.' When she doesn't reply, just stares at him blankly, his consideration stalks to the walls. Their seams are glistening with a fresh coat of paint. There is a synthetic smell in the room, slightly objectionable. The open window lets in stringy ghosts of winter air. This room is spare, a place for abandonings – a bicycle with tyres flat from disuse, pictures not handsome enough to hang, a bookshelf gap-toothed as a catacomb. Everything has been gathered in the centre of the room and half-heartedly draped with a sheet. The walls remain largely a shade of lake-green, but the paint in the tray is the type of blue approved by youths, a colour that reminds him of school days. 'Why are you changing the colour?' he asks, and his tone is surly because something inside him thinks that she should have consulted him. She knows that he loves this house, what it means to him. He likes nothing better than shutting the front door behind him, being here, beyond reach of every day. Change exiles him, shakes his footing. He imagines himself propped in a corner alongside the bike, the sag-sided suitcase, his necessity come to an end. It smarts that her life would go on without him.

'For the dog.' She says it simply, as though it's an obvious thing. 'I read that dogs live in a world that's mostly blue and yellow. They can't see red – that's grey to them. They can't see green – they see green as yellow. But they can see blue. So I'm painting blue. I want him to see things as they are.'

He smiles, very cordially. The dog in question had been dozing on the lawn when he arrived, belly up to the sky, umber eyes fluttering. It had greeted his arrival with an insolent yodel of distaste. He says, 'But I'm sure I've heard somewhere that there are colours people and dogs can't see – colours only insects and reptiles and birds can see. So you can paint the room blue, and we will see it and so will a dog, but none of us could be sure we're seeing things exactly as they are. An eagle might fly into the house – a tarantula or a crocodile might crawl in here. What will they see?'

'. . . I don't know. Maybe I'll paint another room for them.'

'You should. You're like a little redback. You're my vulture, my snake. Paint your bedroom like a lair.'

She lifts her chin, watching him; then lowers her gaze, turning the brush in her hand. It's a good brush, expensive, and it needs to sit in water. There's a prickling behind her eyes, a tearing of the fringe; she feels made of broken china, of gravel spilling to the ground. She has counted down the days to his return, and this is not how she'd imagined it – yet she cannot say she is surprised. These days their encounters – even their reunions – are like battles with small daggers, both of them trying to defend themselves, to clutch their wounds, to inflict injuries that prove how much they're suffering. She feels a jag of unutterable sorrow for what they've lost – the honeyed moments in clandestine corners, the babbling-brook excitement and fervour of it all. It is terrible to recall the days, long ago, when he would phone her three times and then ring again; when he'd risk life and limb for her. When he wanted her so badly that he forsook the man he was. She won't talk of that time, she won't cry. She looks down at herself, unwashed, undecorated, ram-shackle in stale clothes, and the sight makes her darkly smile: all the months of effort to look better than she is have been wasted in these last few minutes. He must be repulsed by what he sees, but maybe it doesn't matter anymore. She draws a brave breath, blinks through rat-tails of hair. 'I have waited and waited to see you again,' she says. 'I missed you – I still miss you – I will always miss you, when you're gone. Are you angry that you came back?'

'No.' The word barely makes it out of him – a gate opens, a rampart falls, blood gushes with a roar. He sinks to his knees, lays the paintbrush aside, brings her to him in his arms. 'No,' he says, 'never, never. I missed you; I thought of you every day. I couldn't wait to see you again.'

To be held by him is the only thing she really needs,

the only thing she wants from this existence. She nestles into his body, asks him plaintively, 'Then why are you always angry with me? Why do you seem to hate me?'

Such heartbreak is rising in him that he whimpers, squeezes her to him, tries to shelter against her insufficient frame. 'I'm not angry, I don't hate you.' He is desperate that she believe him. 'I will never be angry with you. I'm sad, that's all. I'm sad for how things are. Sad for you, sad for me. Sad that everything can't be different.'

'Everything could be different.' She speaks into his chest. 'But nothing will be.'

He holds her, cradles her, his lips pressed to the point of her ear. She is as brutal as a beast, she walks through a world in which everything is starkly apparent. He wonders if she has ever been able to blind herself to a single, arctic truth. 'You know why, don't you?'

'Yes,' she says. 'Because some things are more important than others.'

'But you are important.' He tells her as quickly as he can: he sits back and stares at her. 'You are what lulls me to sleep, and wakes me up in the morning. You are the race of my heart. You're like cool water, you're a bell, you

———

are something I'm running and running to catch. You are the most lovely, the best, the brightest thing.'

She smiles charily; she can't look at him. She knows the brightness he speaks of is something that gleams only passingly – he knows it too, she's sure. He knows such temporary luminance isn't worth the loss of anything. It's like starlight: it's glorious, it silvers the air, but it only exists because a fiery heart is destined to implode or explode. Even now its lustre is dimming, even now he speaks less of something he's feeling than of something he used to feel. 'One day you'll forget me.' She states it blandly. 'One day I'll be gone from you.'

He shakes his head. 'That won't happen. That day won't come. I'm trying to be good – I would leave you, if I could – but nothing's good without you. You might leave me one day, you probably will – but I will never leave you. And I would never forget you, no matter what. I would never forget what we had. You are part of me now, inside.'

Her fingers move faintly over his face. 'You will leave today. Tonight, you won't be here. You always leave. Every time you come here, you go away again.'

He winces, clutching her. 'You know that's how it has

to be. You said you understood. When all this started, I remember you saying you didn't want to keep me.'

She thinks about this, tracing the sleek bone of his jaw. He is exquisite, this man – his beauty, his boundlessness, the vast elation and biblical woe that come as a parcel with him. He is the finest of blades, he is satin and slate, he is a bleed under skin. 'Yes,' she concedes, 'I remember. I said I would never put you in a cage.'

Her touch tickles: he grips her hand, searches her eyes. 'I know it hurts you when I'm not here – when I won't come to you. I know it hurts to think of me being some- where you can't and mustn't come. I know you're alone, I know you need me: and I'm sorry I can't be with you. But I hope you know that I never forget you: that wher- ever I am, you are with me.'

'Am I?' she asks.

'But that's all I can do. It's not much; it might not be enough for you. But for me, it's this or nothing. Things won't change – they can't change. I owe you: but I owe others too. So this is the best I can do.'

After a pause she says, 'You don't owe me. You don't owe me anything.'

———

'Tell me to go,' he urges. 'You should. This is unfair to you. Kick me out and don't look back. Find somebody who can love you properly.'

She touches his lips, breathes in his breath. 'Yes, I should. And if I could, I would. But that's not how I am. I can't love just anybody – I hardly love anyone. I don't love you because I've got nothing better to do. I love you because I can't help it. If you go, I'll still love you. If I told you to go, I would only be saying it because I love you.'

He kisses her fingers, holds her, wants to weep or hum. Into her hair he whispers, 'Don't. Don't tell me to go – not today. Maybe this can be enough, for today.'

She bends into him, this body that seems made for hers, this man whose voice she adores, whose face she can't turn from, this complicated, capricious, cinnamon-sharp being. He has enemies, she knows; he has vanity and a cruel streak; wit and humanity; he has a boyish, girlish chuckle. Her friends will be disgusted, and maybe she is a fool, but she thinks she can exist in the shade for this man. If he loves her as he says he does, then she can thrive in the shade. 'This can be enough,' she says. 'To be with you sometimes is better than never being with you at all.'

———

He laughs, with true relief, into her paint-tipped hair. She is more than he deserves. Without her, he can't think what would make him different from any man trudging the street. She will always be a rare thing, worth capturing – but not him. He fears that he will soon be old, that the breeze is dropping out of his best years. But she has made him special, convinced him of a value he was never certain he had. And for this he does love her: he always will. 'You smell,' he says, because suddenly he's aware of it, and he wants to make her laugh. 'These clothes stink!'

She does laugh. 'They're my work clothes – they're sweaty –'

'Take them off! They offend me.'

'. . . All off?'

'All! You're horrible.'

So she loosens his embrace and sits up straight, pulling first the crumpled windcheater over her head, then slinging her bra into a corner. She shakes off her trousers and underwear without standing; her feet are already bare. She reclines before him naked in the shortest amount of time, haunches and palms on the floor, knees bent and parted. A network of violet veins glows through the skin of her breasts; tendrils of pubic hair are sinfully black against her thighs. This is how he sees her – a naked little witch. These are her exact colours – petal-pink, hibiscus-red, relic-of-summer brown. Nothing else on earth sees these tones of her, no insect, no reptile, no bird – only he. He wants to touch her nipples, then realises that he may. He shuffles close and lifts her left breast, takes her nipple into his mouth and massages it. His cock is probing the barrier where his belt clinches his jeans. He needs to fuck her: the joy is that she will let him. He is in no great hurry, he'll lick her from foot to brow. He won't enter her until he's fucked her with his fingers, his tongue, his toes. This room of unwanteds is not romantic, however, and he doesn't want paint on his clothes. He scoops her up and strides down the hall with her, a nude protesting girl with kicking feet and spotted hands, arms clasped at his shoulders, a sheen of kisses on her breast.

One rainy afternoon she says to him, 'I bought you a present.'

A twist of frustration crosses his face. She knows he prefers to leave empty-handed, the same way he arrives. Occasionally he takes from her kitchen an apple, a fistful of cashews, a slice of fresh bread – small things that are vanished by the time he steps back into the real world. He wants nothing from her except what is most intangible. 'I wish you wouldn't,' he says, because he is dismayed. He can't help feeling that she gives him things because she wants to own him.

She pauses: he thinks she is incredibly stupid, that she fails to understand the simple rules of this game. She is amazed by his flintiness, the towering heights at which he ruthlessly places his own concerns. He is like a bug or a predator in that regard. She asks, 'Do you want to see what it is?'

He doesn't – his curiosity is not the slightest degree piqued – but he is remembering he is a guest here, he is reining in his manners. He doesn't mean to be thoughtless; he wonders when he became so spoiled. 'Yes,' he says, and puts cheerfulness on his face. 'Show me.'

She smiles, a touch suspiciously. 'You'll like it.'

'I'm sure.' He's sure he won't. He watches her step nimbly from the bed to the chest of drawers and fish from amongst her underwear his ominous, unwanted gift. She hasn't bothered to wrap the thing, but it comes in its own clear plastic case. He shakes his head at the sight of it, almost laughing, almost spluttering, backing into the pillows. 'No,' he says. 'No, no, no.'

'Yes.' She crouches on the bed breathlessly close to him, the way a cat comes impossibly close. Naked, like a cat she's a combination of forks and curves. He catches a whiff of her brothy scent and thinks of peat, mangrove swamps, a cauldron: her cunt is a brew of potent things dug from the soil and severed from mummified rodents and plucked, on moonless midnights, from the branches of century-old trees. Hers is the aroma that must have filled the primordial air when there was nothing but bogs and fenland, clotted skies, blue dragonflies.

He draws up his knees to protect himself. 'It's very nice. Thank you. You can put it back in the drawer now.'

Her eyes are glimmering. 'Don't you want to try it?'

'On me? No.'

She chuckles, eyes fringed with long lashes. 'How about on me?'

He hadn't thought of that. She's such a bossy thing. He realises quite abruptly that through all these months, all these disjointed nights and afternoons, he has always thought of things as being done *to* him, not by him – the story, always, about him. He hesitates, from habit; then takes the case from her hands. The latch torments him momentarily, as basic things unfailingly do; when the lid falls back he lifts the thing from its place and is surprised by its presence and substance, heavier than he'd expected. He's never held such an object, never touched one. It is a simple design, an unornamented phallus, perfectly smooth

———

in the shank, steeply rounded at the peak. It's a single colour, a deep mourning-purple. He knows one can purchase all kinds of monstrosities, and he's glad she opted for restraint. 'How do you turn it on?' he asks, for there is no obvious switch.

Her fingers duck under his wrist and pivot the thing's weighted base, and it reacts by buzzing with such animation that he almost drops it – almost releases it to let it bounce free around the room. Its vibration shimmers through his palms and up his arms, pools in his elbows, wasps to his chest. It makes a busy sound, neither quiet nor loud, a rattle-toothed battle song. She is watching him intently, pink-cheeked with amusement. 'Do you like it?' she asks.

He answers, 'Lie down.'

She leans back on her hands, her arms very straight, spreads her legs and inclines her arse to him. Her cunt is an origami of flesh that gapes as her knees separate; florets of tissue, ugly as oysters, bloom with the intricacy of a rose; her tiny hole winks at him. It's a place made for skin, for something alive, but the phallus is buzzing, and his cock has grown hard. He wants to do this, unexpectedly: he wants to shaft this thing into her. He tucks himself around her hips and thigh, so he may hold her but still see. When he touches the tip of the dildo to her she chirps with laughter, kicks a foot. It slides into her easily, two smoothnesses come together: he feels passing disgruntlement that she is as wet for this, this plastic offence, as she always is for him. He feeds the vibrator into her and draws it out lingeringly, and its purple flank spangles with a slathering of her fluid. He pushes it up, feels the dead-end of her, the private place that is shaped for him, and resents this thing being where he alone may be. Her foot finds his cock, her toes jog his tight balls. He plunges the dildo into her quickly, dashing it in and out, rotating it, angling it to her anus, skewering her with its stiff comic length. He likes it, this ridiculous thing. It is a small but gratifying power in his hands. Her foot ferrets between his legs, her instep nursing his balls; she plucks at his pubic hair with long agile toes. He watches the dildo disappear and it's frightful to imagine it in her, he does not want it there; yet he draws it out only to need, again, the sensation of feeding it into her. He's a child who cannot resist doing something he knows he shouldn't do. He smells the vibrator's man-made newness, her female millenniums of age. She's giggling and twitching, but when he glances at her he sees no drowsy contentment in her eyes. 'Do you like it?' he asks.

'I like that you like it,' she answers.

His hand slows; the dildo idles to a halt inside her. This is what he can claim as his own: the happiness that glazes her eyes when he fucks her. When it is his flesh forging a path into hers, when it's his body holding her down, his breath fluttering her hair, his heart knocking her ribs. He eases the phallus out of her, shuts it off, lays it aside. He will kiss her, to have things real again, and then he will make love to her.

'Turn around,' she says, and his tender thoughts vanish, instantly he spangles with apprehension. He retreats into the pillows, shaking his head; only his cock stands courageous, always the last to understand. She picks up the dildo, points its damp tip at him. 'I won't hurt you,' she says.

'You will. I don't trust you. You're a devil.'

The words aren't out of his mouth before he regrets them. He meant it as a joke but they both know what's true. He doesn't trust her, not one skerrick. He's never trusted her not to tell the wide world about his visits here; never trusted her not to ask more of him than she's allowed. She lets a few seconds go by so the words turn leaden and lie on the floor like heavy rusted bolts. Then: 'Have I ever hurt you before?'

You are destroying me, he wants to say. Instead he must say, 'No.'

'Then turn around.'

He shifts away from the security of the bedhead, turns his back to her. She runs a hand up his spine and he lowers his face into the pillows, his brow onto crossed forearms; her other hand slips between his thighs and raises his weightless backside. She shuffles nearer on her knees; he closes his eyes and his fists. Her breathing is cool on him. She spreads his buttocks with both hands, exposing the shy pleat of his arsehole; when her tongue strokes across his skin he swallows air, feels a surge of blood stiffen his slumping cock. Her tongue is broad and sodden, supping him; he feels himself gape and clamp and gape a little again. Her legs are folded between his knees, her face pushed into his arse; her hands come up to fondle his cock, caressing the root of him. This is another gift she's given him, he thinks – this cat-cleaning of his anus. He would like to fall asleep like this, his backside in the air, his head on plump pillows, his balls in her palm, her tongue sweeping his hole.

The buzz of the vibrator makes him squeak and wrecks everything. 'Careful,' he begs, because he can't help himself, he is more leery than a virgin. 'Be careful – please –'

She doesn't answer. His eyes screwed tight, unable to watch, he bites his lip when he feels the shivering phallus slide into the crevice of his buttocks. She touches its tip to his arsehole and inside he is haywire with fear – but the vibrator moves on, he feels her tongue again, tender and infinitely welcome. She is close to him, her knees between his, her breasts firm at his thighs: the dildo, droning calmly, tours his cock and balls, trembles alongside them, whispers eye-to-eye. It explores him, tries to befriend him, shares its joke with him. Meanwhile she licks him, puts her tongue in him, bites him mousily, nibbles his skin. The room is heated; outside it is raining; in his mind he starts travelling, travelling. A sandy landscape, an absence of sound, a balmy breeze at his heels. He has always liked the idea of an oasis – a desert to surround him, a pond of sapphire water, an umbrella of green palm trees, paradise-coloured birds. He would sleep on the grass, his hair blown by fine wind, his shoulders draped with coarse linen. The air would smell of pepper and spices. The ground beneath him would be phosphorescent; at night there'd be infinite stars. His life would consist of nothing but her tongue delving his paths.

He hardly hears the vibrator retire into silence; he flinches only slightly when she runs a finger inside him. Her left hand loops his cock and grips it tidily, begins to pull him so he feels the reach of her through his spine. The finger in him fans a pressure that makes him think of his landscape, the sun and grainy dunes. Her hand moves faster, rougher, her finger jabs in and out. He'd run through the desert with a dog at his heels and he'd lift his chin and howl, a wolf; 'Fuck me,' he says, 'Fuck me.' She drives her tongue into him, fast, dripping, pummels his balls, crushes his cock in her fist. His come leaps out of him in two, three gamy spurts; he cries into the pillows and the white world spins round; when he blinks his eyes open the desert is the bed, the trees are venetian blinds, the sand is cotton sheet. There is no moon or sun – only she sits beside him, soundlessly as he slows to a standstill, strung alone between a couple of worlds.

He lets himself in with his own golden key, its teeth like the Himalayas, jagged and unpredictable, capped with yellow light. The house is stuffy, the window blinds closed; in the loungeroom her dog raises its head from the couch and blinks drowsy eyes at him, flips a plume of tail. He stands in the centre of the room, thinking she might be hiding: she often plays games with him. She sends him cryptic messages, pretends confusion when he knows she understands. She'll give him prank phonecalls, hide chocolate frogs in the toes of his shoes. She'll have no underwear beneath her jeans or shirt, so his wayfaring hands get shocked; one day she opened the front door wearing no clothes at all. When he kisses her he'll taste something

———

tangy, smell something edible dabbed on her skin. Once, he remembers, she shaved herself naked as a kid, and he hadn't known what to say when she had asked if he liked it. He did like it, and that seemed somehow perverse: but he couldn't keep his hands off her, couldn't get enough of that prickleless simplicity against his palms. He looks about himself, smiling, searching; the housekey he slips into his pocket. He had baulked when she'd given him the key, an ordinary thing of little substance that was nonetheless bulky with meaning, a perfectly harmless object he could hardly dare to look at. Now, though, the key feels valuable, in a way he can't explain. The key is freedom. It feels like trust. Like a jewel, it needs a hiding-place. It can be tucked up a sleeve, flung over a shoulder, dropped down a stormwater drain, left behind on a table.

She's not hiding: she is balled up in her bed, occupying a corner near the bedside table. She says his name and he crosses the hall to her, his forehead creasing because he sees immediately that things aren't as they should be. He sits on the mattress at her knees, runs his hand over her face. Her skin is moist, her lips are ashen. Beside the bed is a parched glass and a book, discarded, butterflied on the

———

floor. She has the flu. He smooths down her hair. 'Why didn't you tell me?'

She shrugs, the sheet lifting. 'You wouldn't have come.'

He frowns severely, as if this is wounding, despite the fact that it's true – had he known she was ill, he wouldn't have made the long drive out to see her. There's nothing he can do for her – he can't be a lover, won't be a nurse. Had she told him the facts he would have said, *It's difficult at the moment. I've got a lot of work to do. I'll ring you this evening, if I can.* And now he feels tricked, misled, that she's taken advantage of his ongoing hankering for her. *Emotional blackmail*, he would call it, except he's uncertain if one can blackmail by saying nothing, if emotions can be evoked in circumstances so physical. He should not have come; he should go. Sometimes the entire situation is just too cripplingly fraught, and the smart thing to do would be to go. But she rubs her nose with a palm, blinks glassy eyes at the wall, and suddenly he feels himself plunged into pity for her, lying on her unwashed bed and tending to herself, no one to talk to, the drab days continuing without her. 'I'll get you some tablets,' he says.

———

'Some water.' Maybe he will change the bedding, help her into the shower. He goes to the kitchen, finds painkillers and takes them to her, goes back to the kitchen and brews a pot of tea. He lets the dog out into the yard, refreshes its drinking water, finds a tin of food in the cupboard and knifes it into the animal's bowl. He wipes the bench and rinses clean some dishes. When he returns to her bedroom with two steaming mugs she is lying as he left her, her hands limp near her face. 'Can I hop in?' he asks.

Her eyes flicker fondly to him: 'Of course.' Her voice is rasped, her smile exhausted. He takes off his boots and socks and jeans, pulls his shirt over his head. He hesitates before slipping his underwear down his legs – it hadn't seemed decent to enjoy her shaved cunt, and now it does-n't seem right to force nakedness onto somebody clearly ill. But he dearly wants to be undressed next to her, to feel the camaraderie between flesh. They are at their best when there's nothing between them, no words, no evasion, when they are two ordinary creatures reduced to merely them-selves. It is the time he feels haloed, clad with humble magnificence: the time when he still feels a tumbling love for her. Under the blankets he settles beside her, his fingers on her heated skin. She stretches her legs and lets herself subside. He kisses her nose, her fever-dry arms. 'I'll stay with you,' he says. 'I don't want you to be alone.'

She blinks into the pillow, saying nothing; her eyes are watery with the relief of having him here. He reaches to the bedside table for his tea and doesn't notice that she's crying. In the middle of the morning she had woken, her heart beating like a wing, smothered by the panic inspired by a lucid, concise dream. She had stood at the front door of her house and seen the plants she's raised hacked to the ground, the fence she's built lying in pieces, the earth piled with soot and stone, the garden churned to a wasteland. Reeling with grief, she had stormed at the workmen standing around that they must return everything to the way it had been. One of them had answered her jeeringly: *This is the least of your worries.* He'd waved a smug hand and she had turned to see her home collapsing like a house of straw, disappearing into a flood of stinking livid water that had already engulfed the yard; the trees stood out of the sewage pocked and bent with disease. When she shuts her eyes she sees it again, the frothing sludge around her ankles, the leering faces watching her. It is not a subtle dream. It's a dream that shouts at her. She reaches under the sheets for a touch of him, curls her hand inside his own. She's alone in her stupid love for him, even her subconscious taking a stand against her. Maybe even he thinks she is possessed by a kind of madness that splashes around his ankles too, tainting him, repulsing him. He's told her that sometimes he is nauseated by the guilt inspired in him after he's been here. He has told her that he's wept into his hands, that there have been times when he has loathed himself with a brittle hardness like shale. When her name has made him want to gag, to gouge his heart from his chest. Not now, though: now he is whispering, 'Little one. My poor one.'

She draws him as close as he can be, stowing herself into his lap. Steam rises from her untouched tea as whittled, waltzing wraiths. 'When I was little and I was ill,' she says, in a purly, elderly voice, 'I would sit on the diningroom windowsill, hiding behind the curtain.'

'Why? Were you frightened of going to the doctor?'

'No, it wasn't that . . . I think I was frightened of being sick. I thought it was a bad thing, a naughty thing. Something I should be embarrassed by, the state I'd got myself into, the mess I might make. I think that's what I was: humiliated.'

He sees it, a tiny mousy-haired child perched on a windowshelf with her arms around her shins, drapes of curtain surrounding her, towering to the ceiling above her. Her ears tuned to the approach of her mother, her cheeks blanched with malady and shame. Years later the girl would hesitate to have sex with him when she had her period, citing the very same reason – the mess she might make. He'd laughed – *don't be silly* – and did not mention that he found it arousing, the idea of fucking her while she bled. 'I thought you were hiding today,' he tells her now. 'I wish I could have found you sitting behind the curtains.'

She chuckles into her pillow, and tears drop one after another onto her pillowcase and span out into stars. He catches some before they fall, smears them to nothing between his fingers. 'Don't cry,' he says. 'I'm here.'

'Yes,' she sighs. 'Thank you.'

'Won't you drink your tea? A sip? It will make you feel better.'

She nods as if she will do that, but doesn't reach for her mug. She asks, 'Is tea your favourite thing in the world?'

———

'Hmm, yes, I think so.'

'Better than laughing? Better than the ocean? Better than falling asleep?'

'Better than anything,' he assures her. 'What about you? What's your favourite thing?'

'Kittens,' she says, without hesitation. 'Kittens are my favourite things.'

He smiles, reminded of kittens. One day he will ask her which colour, flavour, number, movie, painting, building, planet and book she likes better than any other. Not today, though. His mobile phone is on the bedside table – with the press of some buttons he sets the alarm to bleat in an hour. He relaxes around her, closing tired eyes, his arms sheltering and reassuring her, her breathing restful now. The tea will go stony; in an hour he'll make some more.

———

They go to a party on the top floor of a grand old building that has been specially hired for the night; the type of exclusive stylish occasion where everyone is well dressed and shyly brings their invitation, where the young men behind the bar are paid to be there and raise their eyebrows when memorising requests, and pour with showy swagger. It is as though the party is being held in honour of the two of them, for in a few days' time it will be exactly one year since he lay himself down on her bed and thought of the sea and of drowning while her fingers traced a pattern like music onto his back. A year later, he still wonders if he can't somehow un-go there, to her house and blue bedroom, un-lie there on her crimson bed,

———

be untempted and undrawn; she wonders if it hasn't been the worst year of their lives. And yet, in this year, they have lived as kites fly. They have lived the pitch and soar and plummet. Together they have gone where they cannot be followed. They have protected each other, hoped for each other, woken for each other, felt the shadow of the other in an otherwise empty hand. They have been, for one another, the nail on which the planet has completed its annual journey around the sun. They know it is not extraordinary.

But even after a year he's cautious: he never forgets to be wary, like an animal born as prey. He doesn't think it's wise to arrive at the same time. 'Who will notice?' she asks, 'Who will care?', but he knows she is testing him. Anyone could notice – any one of them would certainly care. He sees the rumour escaping from its box and racing like a spider round the walls – sees a thousand heads turning, hears a thousand gasps for breath, an intake of air that would surely buckle his world like a bridge. Yet she, too, is part of his world – she is a boundary: a river or a canyon. She is a spider in an ornate box, exquisite and hideous, a captive to be proud of, never to be released.

––––––

She's showing him her fangs now: he follows her up the stairs because otherwise he'll feel her bite. There are a hundred steps or more. Near the top, hearing a band and many voices, he comes to a sharp halt: she spins to him flash-eyed, ready to be curt. But he frames her chin and kisses her, and she says, 'What was that for?'

'Because I'll want to kiss you at the party,' he says, 'and I won't be able to.'

She falters, smiles goofily, her fingers lace momentarily through his own. She loves the winsome streak in him – no one would guess it existed behind his enamel-cool eyes. She would like the universe to hear she adores him, wishes every person living knew that he has slept against her shoulder. She aches to be allowed to touch him, would surrender all her words in exchange for the freedom to speak his name. The silence she carries to keep him safe drags on her like concrete boots, suffocating as a kidnapper's gag. *The want of different things:* it's a simple and murderous pall cast over the eclipsed half-life they share. It's endured like distance, like long absence, like the fact that sometimes they are furious with each other simply because the screws are turned so

———

tight. 'Come on,' she says, nudging him to the door. 'I love you.'

It's the type of party he attends all the time, the kind to which he must coax himself, where he knows almost everyone and everyone knows him. If such occasions bore him, he would never insult a host by letting it show: he stands with a willow's gracefulness to one side of the room and acquaintances seek him out in twos and threes, he is always laughing and nodding, remembering names, impeccably interested, never alone. For her, it is the kind of event that renders her mutant. Her conversation will be terminal, her clothes outmoded, her hairstyle unflattering, her makeup freakish. She doesn't want him to witness it, and drifts as far as she can. She finds friends and fresh air on the balcony, a waitress who offers her a drink. Out here the music is muffled, no one has to shout. She can see him through a glassed wall, in the corner of an eye. The balcony offers a glamorous view of the twinkling city and its lounging light-lit suburbs, but she has never been impressed by the wide-ranging sight of anything. Details please her – she'd rather peek into an exclusive world than be bullied by a mighty spectacle. She sees a parade of ants crossing a footpath, scratches on a car's paintwork, the flawless symmetry of his lips. Flying-foxes cut through the grizzled sky and she sees their keyhole noses, their goatish eyes. She listens to arguments, admires outfits and sympathises, considers a new baby's name. She's asked questions, and answers. None of it is what she cares about. She glances through the glass at him – only him. Her eyes find him in a second. She remembers the many months when she couldn't abide speaking about anything except him – when every conversation in which his name couldn't be evoked was a waste of words that instantly tested her tolerance. Now she can speak of other things, but everything is frivolous. Nothing is as important as the leak of sadness in her. She longs to talk, but what would she say? *He loved me once, but he doesn't anymore: I don't know what I am to him now.* It's not something she can share. It's probable that no one will ever know she has seen every scrap of him, her hands have smelt of him, her cat has rubbed his ankles, she's heard him whisper *Open your eyes.* He has a reputation for being aloof – she could rescue him from it, but doesn't. She has discovered, of late, that he is widely admired by women – he doesn't seem to realise it, but one day he will. He will realise and then she will be like juvenilia to him, something amateur and embarrassing in the light of greater conquests, and he won't ever speak of her, he'll be puzzled by what he saw in her.

She finds herself sinking away from the circle of women who have kindly scooped her into their midst. She likes their company, she's grateful, but she has nothing in common with them. They have wages and husbands and children, they walk a well-tramped path that she has never put a foot upon. Sometimes she envies such people, choosing to believe they know happiness. Probably that's not true. What she really wishes is that she had wings – that she could leap to the brink of the balcony and hunch there, a gargoyle, frightening everyone, sweeping a stare over the threatened city and flying away, like the bats, on creaking wings. She would like a tail that lashes, horns and piercing claws, fangs to lick with a scarlet forked tongue, a wolfish, demon's visage.

He wanders out to the balcony in the company of others – she hears his voice, his name spoken, his uncommitted laugh. She wonders if his eyes are on her shoulders, if he notes her isolation and finds it unappealing. A minute passes before he comes to stand beside her. Ignoring the view he says, 'You look beautiful.' And it's true – sometimes she does. 'Come with me.'

She puts down her glass and follows; she doesn't ask where they're going. He leads her through the crowd to an ancient door propped open with a brick, through this to a small circle of room and a set of narrow stairs that rise steeply, and still she says nothing. He beckons her to climb, and she does. It never crosses his mind that she might fear heights. They climb and climb, she first, he second, standing aside on a landing when they meet a group of partygoers descending, exchanging forced greetings with them. The staircase spirals, becomes metal, pinches thinly, shudders underfoot. They are climbing a tower. She hadn't known a tower was here, looming behind the balcony and the party – she hadn't noticed its lofty silhouette blocking out the sky. It is as if, magician-like, he has reached into a pocket and produced not a bunch of feathery flowers, but the tottering relic of a fairytale. She climbs quickly, confidently, despite the darkness: there's no light except what starlight slants in the medieval windows. She feels him climbing close behind, knows he'd catch her if she slipped, knowing she won't slip.

At the top of the tower is a hexagonal room with a slatted floor and a row of tall peaked windows; its brown stone walls are pitted with countless grooves and tiny holes. She goes to a window and looks over the night city, sees uncountable lights in sandwiched offices, neon signs winking and strobing, flares of every colour and design. Far below her feet are footpaths woven by festive pedestrians and intersections of wide road busy even now, at this late hour. She sees cars, an altercation, the asp of a distant train. She sees highrise apartments and their dizzy occupants, the blink of an aeroplane's warning lights. It is not the view that the builders of this odd old place could have imagined. It's so high up that the noise of the streets and the party can't be heard, a killing distance to fall – she wonders if a builder ever fell. Silence, pinnacles, moonlight, a kiss: it's something from a storybook. She asks him, 'What's your favourite fairytale?'

He is standing behind her, staring past her, amazed by landmarks. Somewhere out there is his house, its lights. He props his chin on her collarbone, says, '*Rumpelstiltskin*, maybe.'

She smiles. 'Yes. That savage little man.'

'I like *The Frog Prince*, too. The idea of being someone different – better – underneath.'

'Princes aren't better than frogs,' she says. 'I like *The Princess and the Pea*.'

'You would.' He hugs her. 'Anything to complain about.'

But that's not why she likes the story. She likes the idea of being true to oneself. To the very marrow, in every drop of blood and heartbeat, effortlessly being what one was born to be. She presses against him, feels his cock slot into the cleft of her arse. 'What are you doing?' she asks.

'. . . What do you want me to do?'

'. . . I don't want you to forget me.'

'I won't,' he says. 'I will never forget you. And you may never forget me.'

She is wearing a dress, because it's that sort of occasion. He unzips his trousers, pulls her underwear to her knees, finds her cunt easily, drives himself in. She gives a little yelp of incredulousness, yaps a laugh at the view. She holds herself steady against the stone as he thrusts, catching her breath every time. Her damp thighs are a sticky friction as he glides back and returns. 'What if I die?' she murmurs. 'Can I forget you then?'

He shakes his head against her. His arms are clasping her shoulders. With every push he feels the gorgeous vault of her, a smoothness like milk, the sure capture of his balls inside his strictured skin. He's aware of everything, a tightrope walker, pinpointedly alert to his very core – at the same time he's almost deaf, almost dumb, reduced to nothing but heart lungs stomach cock, the essentials for staying alive. 'What if I fall through the window?' she's saying. 'Can I forget you on the way down?'

'No.' His thrusts lift her to her toes. She wobbles, digs her fingers in the stone, wonders if this is the reason it's pitted. 'What if I grow horns and fly away?' she suggests. 'Can I leave you behind?'

'No,' he mutters. Inside him, the rushing has begun. Nothing can be changed now. She feels him strive higher within her, the perceptible tensing of his body: her spine bends to meet him, she pushes herself against him, he will not go alone. How nice it would be, to fly away with him.

———

To reveal her true gargoylehood and for him to still say, *I do*. 'I love you,' she says hoarsely, but his concentration is wrapped in her elastic interior, in the birds that are rising through him, in the come streaming up from the depths of him and spearing into hers. He slumps on her, panting, barely dredging the strength to snare himself inside his trousers and straighten her tousled dress. She rests her forehead on the window, feeling already the creeping of fluids. The glass has misted with their breathing, and she wipes it clean with a fist: through this moist peephole she looks down, down, onto the city where she has lived her entire life. She shared the streets and buildings with him when she never knew he existed, but she's unsure if she can do that now – if she won't always hopelessly search the streets for him, if these buildings won't become memorials to him, her unkeepable beloved. He is not going to be hers; he won't choose her above anyone. She will lose him, not *if* but *when:* she is the living past. She still believes that she could thrive in the shade of his life – but he will never flourish while she lingers there, he will always be tailed by a cancerous fear. And one day, to save himself, he will disown her: not if, but when. 'I love you,' she says again, but he has lifted his head to the sound of voices, has stepped away at the clatter of feet on the staircase. He never hears her say those words anymore. *If you don't mean it, don't say it*, she'd once told him, and he had stopped, saying it and hearing it; she can't remember precisely when. 'The Ugly Duckling,' he murmurs: his gaze is fixed on the tremoring stairs as if he expects trolls or ogres or goblins or witches to hook their hideous hands round the railing and raise their awful heads through the floor. '*The Ugly Duckling* is good, too.'

She is calm. He feels like he is being forced through a shredder. 'How long?' he says.

'Six or seven weeks.'

'How long have you known?'

She pouts a lip. 'A few days. A week.'

A week.

'Have you been to the doctor?'

'Yes,' she says.

So it's true. Yet he knows she takes pills – he has seen them in their package, self-contained orange faces in tidy short rows. 'How did it happen?' he asks, forlorn.

She shrugs, laughs subtly. 'A miracle?'

They're out on the back veranda of her house, over-

———

looking the garden. She is standing at the banister, con-templating the view, watching birds and frowning. Maybe part of her mind is digging, snipping, hacking swags of leaves. He is sitting on the wooden bench beside a coffee cup. His legs feel wobbly, his spine a snappable twig, he might never stand straight again: but she could probably climb the tallest tree to gaze into the magpie nest that hangs rangily from the bough. He has a bitten jam biscuit in his hand, an inedible puck; his throat is clogged with shortbread. When he swallows some coffee it's lukewarm, almost cold. Despite all this it's a lovely day. 'It's your deci-sion,' he says.

'I know.'

'I haven't the right to tell you what to do.'

She looks at him. 'You have the right to say what you'd prefer.'

He blinks at his biscuit and coffee, the surface of the beverage congealed into pallid islands. She always makes it too weak for him. An insect is walking the crest of the cup's handle, a nondescript miniature gnat. He prefers the life he was living three minutes ago – he remembers it as being carefree as a cat's – but he can't say the necessary words. 'Whatever you want. I'll agree to what you want.'

Her bare toes are scuffing the planks of the deck, her elbow creased on the banister. She hasn't touched her own coffee. 'Well,' she says, 'I've made an appointment. For next week – I couldn't get one sooner.'

'. . . Is that what you want?'

She pouts again, as if it's nothing to her. 'It's what has to be done. You say it's my choice, and that's kind of you, but it has never been my intention to cause you pain. I know you haven't believed that sometimes, but it's true. I have only ever wanted you to be happy. And this would pain you, I know. I know it's not what you would want. But you would feel obliged. And you would feel tricked – you would feel like you'd been trapped –'

He interrupts. 'Don't worry about me. Do what *you* want to do.'

She sighs, not dolefully. 'I don't want to trap you. I don't want you in my life just because you can't escape. That's no life for anyone.'

He considers her – she looks no different than she

always does, in these moments when everything could change eternally. He regrets all the loneliness he's caused her, he regrets ever crossing her path; he regrets that, so far, he hasn't been able to let her go. And he could kiss her for being as strong as she is: she's iron, she's granite, she's mighty. Maybe he has never known anyone so remarkable. 'You don't cause me pain,' he says. 'Whatever we've been through, the pain has never been you.' She watches him speak, then smiles fadedly, looks away across the lawn. The work of a garden is unending, trim, hoe, bury, mow. 'I'll come with you,' he says, feeling gamer, the beat tentatively returning to his heart. 'I'll pay.'

She shakes her head. When she came to this house there was nothing, just a few ill-assorted trees. Now there's grass, garden beds, secret corners, paradise. A hot hillock of compost, dirt tracks carved by the dog, a swing roped to a high branch. There have been more flowers this spring, fewer aphids, heavier rains; in the air she feels the approach of a blistering summer. 'No, it's all right.' The next storm will bring down the dying eucalypt limb. 'I'll go alone. I'd rather.'

———

'Well, I'll pay. Just tell me how much it costs.'

She says flatly, 'It doesn't matter.' The cost is incalculable, inconceivable. She sees that blackbirds have dug out a row of seedlings and left them to wither on the soil. 'I shouldn't have told you.' She doesn't look at him. 'I wasn't going to. But I think it's fair you should know. You deserve to know. I didn't want to do anything behind your back.'

Now he's safe, he can be sorry. He can afford to be rueful for what will not be. He imagines not a clutch of cells, a horror-faced tadpole, but a small sprightly child, flute-voiced, elf-chinned, flighty-haired and fawn-limbed, a child who would inherit its mother's love of wild things, its father's need to be close to the sea. A boy or girl – a girl is what he'd prefer. But he would never be able to speak her name, never show her off to neighbours and admiring shopkeepers. He couldn't write her birthday on the calendar or wait outside her school. He could buy her dresses and baby dolls but only in secret, armed with a mouthful of lies. He couldn't teach her to ride a bike or to tie her laces, could never laugh at her misdeeds on parent-teacher night, never pick a path between rockpools with her. 'I couldn't be a proper father,' he says.

She says nothing in reply; her fingers drum the banister. Her own father had been absent, a remote withdrawn man. In the past days she has fretted ceaselessly, but she has never for one second doubted that, if she wanted to, she could do this alone.

Her silence ghosts by him unnoticed, he's distracted by the vision of ribbons and plastic jewellery, of socks with shell-pink bows. A little child with a name, a gap-toothed smile and a favourite toy, eyes as blue as sky. He sees with sudden clarity what it is he's party to, and it pushes his back to the wall. He wants no part in deciding anyone's fate. 'Are you sure it's mine?' he says. 'Are you sure you're asking the right person?'

She turns to look at him, and so does her world – the trees crane, the sun swings its rays, the worms pause in their tunnelling, the birds alight and peer. 'Who else's would it be?' she says, and there's ice in her voice, vastness. Insects have lifted their bead-like heads, the grass has stopped growing. 'What is it you're saying?'

And he feels the beginning of an endless fall between

———

glaciers, the frigidness that will soon encase him. His hackles rise, as they always do when he knows he is endangered, when he is ashamed. 'I don't know,' he answers. 'I don't know everything about you.'

'You don't know I love you? I haven't told you often enough?'

'Yes, you've told me. But I don't know what you do when I'm not here.'

She stares at him, her vision blurring as if she's been dealt a violent blow to the head. Her love for him has blocked all else from her sight: every man is his inferior, every touch that isn't his makes her recoil. She knows he lies to her, avoids her sometimes; she knows she runs her fingers through just the surface of his life. But that is not how it has been for her. She has drenched herself with him, devoted sinew and bone to him, rocky depths. Any lies she has told have been to shield, protect, and coddle him. Very quietly she replies, 'It's not me who goes home and sleeps with somebody else every night.'

His mouth twists balefully. 'Don't start this. We've been through this. You knew how things were when you met me. You didn't have to do this. Maybe you shouldn't have. Maybe it would have been better. You know things can't change.'

She doesn't wrench her gaze from him; the trees and birds lean closer to hear her reply. 'I know you don't want things to change,' she says. 'I know you want what you already have. I know I would give everything to you, but there's nothing I have that you want. I know I've made a fool of myself. I know it's stupid to love someone who has had to learn to like you in return.'

His eyes narrow, affronted. 'Even when I said I loved you, you never believed me. How do you think that felt?'

'I never believed you because it was never true.'

'Fine.' He puts down the cup and biscuit. 'If that's how you feel, why am I here? Why do you talk to me? Why do you let me fuck you?'

Tears have gathered in her eyes, but she will never cry in front of him again. 'A little of you has been better than nothing,' she says; and she knows it is pathetic, she wishes she were a tree or a bird, something that is never contemptible, some proud being that would rather drop dead on the ground than betray itself so cravenly. But he

———

has hardly heard, he's hearing nothing, there's white noise garbling in his head. He looks at his watch, winces theatrically, gets up in a hurry. He's never wanted to flee somewhere as desperately as he needs to quit this place. He's still falling, falling, all he can see are frozen ice walls rushing by him, racing away above him, the sky a sleety needle-thin sliver now. 'I've got to go,' he says. 'I'm late for a meeting. Stay here, don't see me out. I'll phone you tonight.' And later he'll think he should have added other things, just a few unimportant things.

When he is gone and she can no longer hear his car, she takes the cups inside to the kitchen, rinses them and sets them on the drying-rack, and wanders down the hall to her bedroom. Her legs feel very heavy, her skin like transparent tissue, her chest broken blackly open. It is an effort to keep her head up, to haul her feet along. She wants darkness: she would like to go back to the start. As a kid she used to hide under her bed for no reason except the peace of it. She still slips under a bed easily. The casket-like space is dim and cool, consoling. The carpet is unworn and spongy, mysteriously dusty. Her shoulders, slumped, do not strike the underside of the bed. She curls up and lies still, hearing herself breathe. A frosty sound on a sunny day.

Her dog comes into the bedroom, dips his head to gaze beneath the mattress, assesses what he sees. He makes the decision to crawl into the dark space and settle beside her. She puts her face against him, works her fingers through his ursine coat, huddles piteously into his unexpected benevolence. She feels battered, purple and blue. Her skull feels shattered, her throat cut, her eyes gouged and streaming liquid. She won't walk in the park with him, won't help him pick fruit from the trees. She won't go window-shopping with him or watch him sort through the mail. Her lungs feel packed and flooded, her heart wrested from its cave. She won't run down the street after him when he leaves his wallet behind. Her spine is snapped, her ribs are kindling, her teeth are torn from her jaw. Her hands between her pulverised knees are smashed, the fragile bones jigsawed. She'll never see him cooking dinner, won't dry dishes as he washes them. She won't buy him socks or tug his sleeve or put a blanket on him when he sleeps. Nothing will happen. Her stomach aches. The soles of her feet are skinned raw. Her ankles are splintered, her toes ripped away, her nails are seeping blood. She won't grow old with him, won't watch him growing old. Sorrow is purring as it consumes her. She wonders if this is how it's supposed to feel.

But when he rings that evening, she does not answer the phone. He holds the receiver close to his face and tries to feel if she's there, beyond, listening. He lets the phone ring seven or eight times, which is enough to prove she's not answering. Maybe she is in the shower, maybe walking the dog. He rings again later, but still she doesn't pick up the phone.

The next morning he telephones from work, and there's nothing. He stares at the debris on his desk, chocolate wrappers, a junky memento, piles of photographs, his mind coasting. He remembers something she once said: *It's not me you hurt when you say such things. One day, what you say will make me love you less than I do.* Yet he

———

rarely means the things he says. She is angry; and he is contrite, so he will kiss her, comfort her, call himself names. Tell her, again, that it's her choice. It might make his life difficult, but life is difficult anyway. *It's a terrible thing to do to yourself, to make yourself less loved.*

He rings throughout the day, and there's no answer. He picks at dinner that night. He knows he shouldn't worry – it's not her way, to wade in indignation. She pardons, turns a blind eye. He goes for a walk and, passing a telephone booth, he stops to punch in her number. The coins clatter home to him when he sets the receiver down.

The following day, the phone rings and rings. He considers going to her house, but doesn't. If she wanted to speak with him, she would answer the phone. Inside him, wounds like papercuts are opening, small, high-pitched, panicky. He attends to his work, shuffles pages, holds an image up to the light. As the hours grind by, something inside starts to shrill. *To make me love you less than I do.*

The next afternoon he's decided: he gets in the car and drives. There's a sense of homecoming as he opens her gate – it's inexplicable, his love for this house, his sense that it likes him. He feels very welcome; it seems too long since he was last here. There's been rain overnight, and the wet lawn snags his feet. The colour of the weatherboards is the same but somehow different. There is no answer to the doorbell when he rings. He has a key, but he's left it at work – he wants the door opened by her. He goes to a window and looks in, a hand lifted against the light. Between the slats of the blinds he sees her books, her table, the old rug. Her paintings on the wall. Distracted, he mistakes his reflection as being a stranger in the room, raising a fist at him – it makes him take a jerking step back, his heart hectically slamming. This suburb is a cemetery, there's absolute deadness, no neighbours around to ask. He stares into the street, defeated. Maybe she has taken the dog to the park. He could go there, walk across the grass to meet her, but he doesn't know where the park is; and turning to leave he sees what he hadn't immediately noticed, that the garage is empty, her car is gone. Her car is gone, the dog is gone, she isn't answering the phone. She has run away somewhere, to think, to sulk, to punish him. He'll wait.

But one day is a long time to wait, and two are torture.

———

The telephone rings and rings. Sometimes he imagines her pause what she's doing, turn her head and gaze at the phone. Knowing it's him, refusing. That night he dreams of her, naked as a lizard beneath him. He fucks her ferociously, with a clammy kind of ire. Her knees grip his hips, she speaks to him, but her sights keep slipping to something he can't see. In his sleep, he feels himself sliding. He remembers every inch of her, her smoking scent, her snake-smooth interiors, it's a knowledge sunk so deep in him that he'll know it even in the grave. He kisses her, full of love for her, but her eyes keep glancing away. When he wakes, it's to the knowledge that waiting is useless.

In a minute of solitude he dials the number of a business he has seen from the tram, its overlookable premises made obvious by the obstacle-course of pasty men and drawn-cheeked women who gather each morning at the gate, their handmade posters and placards in dingy disrepair. He gives her name and explains the situation, but is told with scalpel-fine courtesy that patient information is confidential. Under no circumstances, no.

He puts the phone down, puts his head in his hands.

Part of him watches himself with canine curiosity,

ears erect, cocking its chin. He tows himself through the mornings, the endless afternoons. At night he watches television and his mind is a featureless plain. Sometimes a terror so monstrous rears in him that he thinks his body won't bear it, he'll be paralysed by anguish; other times he decides he can't genuinely miss her, because perhaps she was right: perhaps he never loved her. If he missed her, if he truly loved her, he would surely feel more desperate than he does. And yet, he can't imagine how much more desperate it is possible to be.

A week of her absence is a landmark like a mountain. Three days crawl by on their knees. He paws through the directory until he finds her surname. Some of the names which surround hers would know her, and maybe know of him. He writes down numbers but accosting strangers seems the act of an hysteric, and he locks the list in a drawer. He stares at the computer screen, unthinking; then pushes out his chair.

He gets in the car and makes, once more, the straight and long journey. Probably he will never travel these suburban roads without thinking of her – there were times he could never drive fast enough, when his fingers would be bloodless at the steering-wheel. Times when he wound down the window to be stunned by a gale.

It is a glorious afternoon, but she is not working in the garden. There are wattlebirds in the shrubs, drably-dressed acrobats bending double over nectar. In the letterbox is a wedge of junkmail. He presses the doorbell and nervously waits. He feels that this time she will answer. The garage door is closed, but he won't lift it to see if her car is there. When she opens the door he will scoop her up, lift her from her feet, hide his face in her hair; he'll cry.

And moments pass, and he presses the bell again, and knows that she won't come. He sinks against the weatherboard, head thumping, hands pulsing. The sun is very dazzling, its glare on the house makes him squint. He wishes he had written a note that he could slide under the door. It strickens him to realise he's never left anything to show that he's been here. Maybe she returns hoping to find something, a flower tucked in the flywire, a reflection lingering in a pane, a message written in chalk on the driveway, and she's disappointed again and again. *Where are you?* he could write, in huge searching letters. *This isn't a story. It has never just been about me.* Small words that might be big enough to bring her back, catch her as she'd once courted him.

He goes to the window, looks in. The room is cleared, the furniture vanished. Her books, her paintings, her desk, her chair; the rug disappeared from the floor.

For a moment he's perplexed – she's redecorating? And then knows.

He crashes through the garden to reach the next window – he doesn't care that branches break and petals shatter, that bees rise humming in aggravation. In her loungeroom he had once lain on a blanket and stared at her naked, upturned. Now the blanket is gone, the couch is gone, the coffee table, the television. He claws his fingers into the glass, a noise coming from him, a strand of plaintive sound. He shoves away from the window and skirts the house to gaze through the window of her bedroom. The bed is gone, the bedside table, the pictures from the walls. The chair in the corner where he threw his clothes. Squares of compressed carpet testify to where the bed used to stand. The cupboard door has been left open, and gapes a shady maw. It's an empty room, just floor ceiling walls door, a vacant box that recalls nothing.

———

His heart is a bird in water, battering wings. He drops to the ground, his back to the wall, his knuckles pressed to his mouth. His mind is scrabbling for an explanation other than the one that's true. *One day I will love you less.* The words are apocalypse, simple; they translate into the end of a world. He sits on the bricks which are crimped with dry moss and knows this is what death is like – sudden death, someone beloved's. A fact, framed in unremarkable terms, that pushes the planet from its course and makes offensive everything that continues to survive.

In the days that follow, his shock will sleek into a resentment that lashes out in every direction, spitting venom, unrestrained. He will throw the list of names and numbers into the bin: she has left without a word, so no one will say anything. Probably she's gone to somebody else – he was far from her first, probably never her only – she was always by nature a creature of deceit. Probably there are no boundaries to the lies she's told. Every word she uttered was crafted to weaken him; every move she made was meant to hurt. She has dissected him, studied him, discarded him. Inside, he is tearing muscle from bone. He deserved better than silence from her. He deserved a farewell equal to all that had gone before – an unravelling, not a slicing, of strings. He deserved, at least, a kiss goodbye. He sits on a city bench and hardly notices how painfully his nails are dug in his skin. What she has done is an act of malice. *I love you less.* Good, he thinks: I'm glad. I am dead to you: I don't love you at all. I'm happy you have forgotten me. Leave me be: don't think about me, don't talk about me, don't say my name. Take your destructive hands, your graveyard voice, your filthy face away. And when he reaches such heights of rage that he can barely stand, he puts his palms to his eyes and cries. He misses her. Her absence is what shakes him from sleep, the first thing he remembers, the last thing he forgets. He wakes each morning already tired, drained by the prospect of another day. And though his life is exactly as it used to be – same people, same places, everything he so frantically feared losing and would have chosen ahead of her – he feels hollowed, ransacked, irreversibly changed.

Summer lies down like a wolf's pelt. At dusk the sky is orange, yellow and pink, the same colours sunk into the swollen fruit he buys. He telephones her house occasionally, and listens to a voice tell him that the number is not

———

connected. He wonders what he'd say if she unexpectedly answered – he has no speech prepared. On the street he watches traffic absently, wanting and not wanting to see her car. If he saw it, he would run. He would leap walls, bound buildings, fly. He scans faces in queues, at markets, in parks, crossing the road. He wonders what became of the small things he gave her – if she took them with her or threw them away. For days he can think of nothing but this, her unknown decision: he presses his fingers repeatedly into the uncertainty, just to feel the sting. He is struck, one day, with the need to have a Christmas present for her, and finds himself buying a bottle of the oil she sometimes dabbed on her wrists. It smells syrupy – like childhood, like lollies chosen conscientiously and dropped into a paper bag. Now the smell is simply her. He asks that the present be wrapped but after a few hours unwraps it, uncaps it, holds the bottle to his nose. And then hides it, like everything else; like half his life.

Early in the new year he goes lacklustrely on holiday, catching a plane to sit on a beach and stare out at the blue sea. *I love you like the sun loves the ocean; I need you like the ocean needs the moon.* She must have said those

―――――

words one day – she always said they talked too much, she, who did most of the talking. In this far-off place she seems far away, more like something he's imagined: yet he never stops following faces, dodging surfboards and seagulls and ice-creamy kids, searching for her somewhere she'd never be. He would know her if he saw her, yet he's aware he is forgetting the details of her. She is fading. Only sometimes, at night, when he sleeps restless under sunburn and an afternoon of wine, he finds that she'll come back to him, sit between his knees, place her hands on his face. 'Why did you leave me?' he asks, like a child. And sleeps with his head on her stomach, hearing the rumble and beat of life in her depths.

In autumn he notices the changing colour of the trees, the thickening of the shadows, the increasing silence of the birds. He rakes the yard and mulches the garden with the sweepings, knowing she would be pleased. He has learned to live with the pit that is her loss, the many things he craves to know. Hours go by without him thinking of her; but never a whole day. Now and then he dials her number, in case. He has thought about driving past the house, but the sight of another car in the driveway, the rampant shrubs chopped into submission, the boots by the door creased to somebody else's feet – these are things he could not bear to see. And yet, increasingly there are times when he fancies everything was only pretend. That the boots were always creased by another, that the garden was some wilderness he glimpsed as a boy. He has everything he had before she cannoned into his life: nothing is missing. If he carries an injury that weeps constantly, it is only small. He cannot stop looking for her, but it is just a habit he will eventually lose. He does not forget her birthday, but he doesn't buy a gift.

But the wound is not small: not in truth. In truth he knows he stepped off a cliff the day he met her, when she fed him that ridiculous line, *I want to screw you till you scream*. In truth he knows he has endured something unfathomable, and that his life will never be as it was. It appears unaltered, to anyone looking in; it is not. Everything is changed, and she is gone, and when he asks *Who am I?* there's no answer, he's no one. He is someone set free. He said the word, and she, keeping hers, let him go.

One day, eating lunch in the park, bundled against the moist encroach of winter, he has a thought that makes him lower his sandwich to his lap. *I love you less*. The words have ached in him for months. The thought that she left because she stopped loving him has lamed him like a badly-healed bone. *It's a terrible thing to do to yourself, to make yourself less loved*. He's dragged the damage behind him like an unadmitted crime. He has hated himself, for making himself less loved; hated her for loving in such a faulty, unforgiving way. But with the cool wind of coming winter blowing by him, he sees what he's been blind to for heartbroken months. Her vanishing was a move to protect him – to place him on a high shelf, away from further harm. To return him safely to the things he did not want to lose. To prove she'd ask for no sacrifices from him. She had gone not because she loved him less: she'd gone because she loved him more.

Leaving him with everything but her.

The story, after all, about him.

He struggles to remember her face; he can no longer summon her voice. He visits friends, swears at traffic, jogs along the river. He cleans his shoes and cuts his hair and goes out for drinks with colleagues. He makes the bed each morning, plumping the pillows, arranging them

———

nicely, smoothing the wrinkles from the sheets. He tries never to think of her. Occasionally some little thing – a particular stride, a quirk of speech, the way a girl covers her mouth when she grins – will return her to him exquisitely, and he'll see for an instant her wonky smile, her scruffed elbows, her well-worn scowl. He'll see her back, the flat planes of her shoulderblades, see her prop her chin on her knee. But mostly, when he thinks of her, what he sees is not her. He sees a bird beating wide strong wings, flying fast and steadfastly very high above the earth. The bird, white as snow or lightning, never pauses, never looks down, ignores his travelling gaze; it cuts through the clouds resolutely, the downstroke of its wings thumping ruggedly against the air. Its dark eyes are fixed unswervingly on the horizon; he's never known something so sure of its destiny. There comes a day when he finally stops searching for her on the ground, amongst the ordinary, and turns his face to the sky.

———